He just kept getting an uneasy feeling that Lily was alone in town and in trouble.

They both stood up at the same time. This close, for that millisecond, he saw a pearl of perspiration on her neck. Saw the tilt of her head, proud, stubborn. Saw the sunset in her hair.

He had to bend down almost a foot to kiss her. Didn't know he was going to do it. Didn't plan it, didn't intend to.

Her face tilted to accommodate the landing of his mouth, not as if she were inviting him, but as if she just instinctively moved to make a meeting of lips more natural, more easy. He tasted ice cream. He tasted the vulnerable satin of her lips.

He lifted his head—almost immediately—saw the startled flush on her cheeks, thought…oh yeah, she was tough, all right.

Tough as a rose petal.

Yet the irony hurt worse than any burn. If, by any chance, she and Griff *did* find the answers…her reasons for being in Pecan Valley disappeared.

She had no more reason to be with Griff.

No reason to stay.

★★★

Dear Reader,

This story has a bunch of elements I love working with—a hero who's not what he seems, a heroine who somehow has to find a way to right an old wrong, characters who have to take scary risks to get what they need in life.

He is *so* wrong for her. She's *so* wrong for him.

What could be more fun?

I hope you enjoy the story!

Jennifer Greene

You can reach me at www.jennifergreene.com or on my Jennifer Greene page on Facebook.

JENNIFER GREENE

Irresistible Stranger

ROMANTIC
SUSPENSE

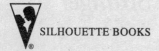

SILHOUETTE BOOKS

Recycling programs
for this product may
not exist in your area.

ISBN-13: 978-0-373-27707-0

IRRESISTIBLE STRANGER

Copyright © 2010 by Alison Hart

This edition published by arrangement with Harlequin Books S.A.

For questions and comments about the quality of this book
please contact us at Customer_eCare@Harlequin.ca.

Visit Silhouette Books at www.eHarlequin.com

Printed in U.S.A.

JENNIFER GREENE

lives near Lake Michigan with her husband and an assorted menagerie of pets. Michigan State University has honored her as an outstanding woman graduate for her work with women on campus. Jennifer has written more than seventy love stories, for which she has won numerous awards, including four RITA® Awards from the Romance Writers of America and their Hall of Fame and Lifetime Achievement Awards.

You're welcome to contact Jennifer through her website at www.jennifergreene.com.

To Lil—just for being so wonderful

Chapter 1

The afternoon wasn't just hot. It was choking hot. Gasping hot. Suck-your-brains-out hot.

Lily Campbell stepped off the curb, feeling the pavement fry her feet even through her thick, cork sandals. It was only two more blocks to the sheriff's office.

She could make it two more blocks without dying, couldn't she? Surely?

She wanted to laugh. She'd been so certain that this trip home to Pecan Valley after twenty years would be horrendously traumatic. Instead, every view so far had provoked a gush of hopelessly happy memories—of her dad pushing her in a creaking swing. Of her sisters shrieking and dancing through sprinklers. Or her being snuggled between her mom and dad on a porch swing, watching the fireflies at dusk.

Somehow, she always remembered the fire. Not the idyllic childhood before it. And for darn sure, she had no memory at all of this killer Georgia summer heat.

She pushed a heap of heavy chestnut hair off her neck, thinking she'd either have to get her long hair cut off or suffer heatstroke, but her real attention focused on Main Street. She passed Annabelle's Bakery, Susan's Secret Treasures, Belle Hair, an insurance office. On the other side of the road, hugging the corner, was Debbie's Diner and a shoe store.

None of the names latched in her memory, yet somehow she remembered other things. A woman with big hair and a white ruffled dress passed by her, nodding a polite hello. An old gentleman snoozed in a white rocker outside a storefront. A couple of giggling girls, sucking on popsicles, window-shopped across the street.

She knew this town. It smelled and tasted and looked like home, even if she hadn't been back since she was eight, even if she couldn't imagine living here ever again. She'd given herself exactly eight weeks…to solve a twenty-year-old crime.

Complicating that problem—just a wee bit—was that no one twenty years ago believed there *was* a crime. Not the police. Not even her sisters. No one.

She'd plotted and planned this trip for almost two years, but back in Virginia the idea had made such sense. She needed to do this. She'd needed to forever. Now that she was here, trudging through this blazing, baking sun, she fully realized that everything about the plan was complete and total lunacy.

A red truck, older than her, stopped at the corner to yield the right of way. The next block echoed the last one. The storefronts were different, but the sleepy, Southern town mood was the same. First up was an old-fashioned pharmacy, then a crafty-type jewelry store—she had to gallop past that one, shielding her eyes, knowing how readily she could sucker into a new pair of earrings. Right now, she'd likely sucker into any conceivable sales pitch to postpone her visit to the sheriff's office.

Lily figured that if a woman was determined to be stupid, there was no point in hanging out half a flag. Might as well go for it all the way. Still, she knew darn well that walking into that old brick building was going to be traumatic times ten.

She ducked under a candy-striped awning, kept going for three steps, then hopelessly, helplessly, backed up. For sure, this place hadn't been around when she was a little girl, because she'd have remembered it. Griff's Secret—Fresh Churned Ice Cream, claimed the sign in the window. The list of flavors for the day included Peachy-Cream, Blueberry-Drizzle, Chocolate-Miracle, Baby-Blue and "as always", Griff's Secret.

She wasn't hungry. And darn it, she hadn't traveled all this way just to back down on a streak of cowardice.

But her right hand seemed to reach out and open the door. Her right foot seemed to step inside. The air-conditioning alone was enough to make her sink to the floor in a grateful puddle. She'd work up her courage again in a few minutes. Right now, nothing in life seemed more important than getting a taste of that ice cream.

* * *

Griff was just trolling the sports section for ball scores when the stranger walked in. Granted, he was always prone to noticing a good-looking woman, but this one snared more than a swift once-over.

The long sweep of lustrous chestnut hair caught his attention first, then the Yankee-white skin that looked softer than a baby's butt. *Soft* pretty much described all of her. She was wearing a pale pink tee, white jeans, cork sandals. He guessed her height around a respectable five-five, nothing heavy about her, but she had distinctly soft edges—plump boobs, a definite cup to her fanny. Lips softer than butter.

Still, it wasn't the prettiness that captured his interest, but the greed. On a scale of one to ten, she was easily a nine, every texture pure female, something about her that radiated sensuality, kindness, gentleness. Offhand, Griff would have pegged her as too goody-good for him, but then her blue eyes narrowed on the ice cream counter. And there it was. Right in her eyes.

A hefty dose of lusty greed.

She didn't notice him. Griff suspected she didn't notice much of anything. Good thing no small children stood between her and the ice cream, because she sprinted across the room faster than a thief in a bank vault.

"Can you tell me what this flavor is?"

She directed the question at Steve behind the counter. Griff had hired the kid when he had no place to go, which was pretty much how he found most of his workforce. Steve was gawky-thin, had two eyebrow rings, a tattoo on his neck and the generic scowl of a delinquent—which he was. He had been kicked out of school three times last year alone. Oddly enough, the stranger with the Virginia accent looked at the boy as if there was nothing unusual about his appearance.

"We call that one Griff's Secret, ma'am. It's everybody's favorite. If you never tried it…well, let's just say, once you've tried Griff, you never go back."

"Hmm. Okay. Could I have a small cone? It has to be the smallest. I don't even have time for that, but it looks so—"

"Yeah, it is, ma'am. Beyond good. Everybody says so."

"How much?" She buried her head in a purse the size of a small country, emerged with a change purse barely big enough to hold a half dollar.

He'd have gone back to his paper—really. Except that, once she got a hold of the kid-size sugar cone, she sank into one of his fountain stools, closed her eyes, and took a single, long, slow lap.

The town claimed no one ever moved slower than Griff Branchard, but it wasn't true. He just believed that speed required motivation. Seeing that soft, pink tongue curl around that cone propelled him across the room in maybe three seconds flat.

"I was hoping you might like that flavor," he said, deliberately making his voice honey slow, because she looked like a lady who could be spooked easily—and he sure as hell didn't want to do that.

Her eyes popped open, and for a whole, long second, she treated him to a dazzling smile. Griff had seen it before. Sometimes he only had a small window of opportunity before a woman slammed on the caution brakes, but invariably, females initially liked what they saw.

Some days, that struck Griff's sense of humor, since it made no sense to him why women would be attracted to scoundrels. When he looked in the mirror he saw nothing particularly interesting, just an ordinary six-three guy who shaved every other day—when he remembered— had his dad's chiseled bones and his mom's sloe eyes, and a head of black hair that never stayed brushed. He owned the small-scale ice cream parlor, as if he didn't have a serious ambition in the universe, never publically got involved in anything meaningful or troublesome—except for women, of course, but a guy had to have some vices. Yet, without knowing a single good thing about him, the women flocked. It was an amazement.

This particular soft sweetie, though, took the dazzle off the smile faster than most. Still, she didn't send him packing altogether. "I take it you're a fan of this ice-cream flavor?" she asked.

"I've kind of been hired by the owner to do the focus group thing. You know. Find out why a customer chooses a certain flavor. Then, whether they're happy they made that choice. And I know what pretty much every kid in town thinks, so it's nice to have someone new, get a fresh opinion." He was in the chair across from her before she could object, and once he'd put out that agenda, she seemed to relax again.

"Well…I chose the flavor because it sounded interesting. And looked interesting. And so did all the others, so I just figured I couldn't go far wrong. But the first taste of this—" Alarmed, she saw a drop of ice cream start to slide down the cone. Her tongue found it faster than a soft little whip.

He was in love. That fast.

Not for the first time. He always fell in love fast, got over it just as fast, but man—she was *adorable*.

"This taste," she murmured, and hesitated. "You just can't know if you haven't tried it. But—"

"Tell me," he coaxed.

"Well...there's a hint of dark chocolate. And vanilla bean. Then a little burst of fruit—like sweet cherry, maybe, or that sweetness in the skin of a ripe purple grape? But there's still something else." She took another lick, closed her eyes, thought. "A crunch. Like maybe just a pinch of almond. It's all there, in the smells, the tastes, the textures. Like putting every fabulous flavor in the universe together in one ice cream. Yet it's subtle."

She looked at him, as if to make sure he wasn't bored by her analysis. He wasn't remotely bored. He was beyond interested. He was prepared to listen to her all afternoon—at least until the kids started piling in.

"Are you in town for long?" he asked.

"Just the summer. I used to live here when I was a little girl. I just came back...to see what I remembered."

"Bring your husband and kids with you?"

She wagged a finger at him. "You're good."

"Beg your pardon?"

"You already looked, so you know I don't have a wedding ring. But I'm only here for eight weeks—for absolute sure, not a minute longer. And I think you'll find, after a few days, that I'm not a friend you'll want to have."

"Come again?"

"I strongly suspect people won't appreciate my being in town. Still. Unless you ask me not to, I'll be back for more ice cream." She stood up, pulled the strap of her purse to her shoulder. "Can I ask your name?"

"You bet, cher. Griff Branchard."

Her eyebrows lifted. "So it's yours? Griff's Secret?"

"All mine. And I'm easy to find, so when you get the urge the next time—well, the next one's on me." He couldn't imagine her doing anything that would offend people. Her eyes were as honest as sunshine; the way she walked and moved was characteristic of a woman easy within herself. Except for the greed and lust thing of course, but that was about temptation. "And you are…?"

"Lily. Lily Campbell."

"You're welcome here any time. Might as well know now that I'm real likely to ask you to dinner one of these days."

"I won't hold you to it," she promised him, and with a smile, aimed for the door.

He almost followed her out, wanting to ask a few more questions—she'd raised more curiosity and interest than he could simply let go of—but then Jason showed up from the back room. Jason was scruffy and scrawny and looked chronically underfed. The kid worked harder than a dog, never back talked, never looked up if he had a choice. The shiner on his right eye was new since yesterday, and he was walking too careful, like something hurt out of sight.

Griff turned away from her and aimed for the kid.

The stranger was pretty and puzzling and appealing, but when push came down to shove…well, there just wasn't a choice. The kids had to come first.

By the time he had a chance to glance back, Lily Campbell was already out the door and had disappeared from sight. But he knew damn well he'd track her down and find out the story before another full day passed.

Recharged and renewed, Lily felt as if she'd gotten her pluck back. Even heading outside into the furnace heat and humidity didn't dent her determination this time. She jogged across the last street and headed up the steps to the old, redbrick police station. Only then did her heartbeat catch up with her, and she had to suck in a gulp of air.

She'd felt alone before. She'd been alone before. When it came down to it, she'd felt alone ever since she was eight years old. Her two sisters meant the world to her… but this was different. Either they didn't remember the fire, or they didn't remember the tragic events of that long ago night the way she did.

She was tired of being haunted.

Quietly, she pulled open the door. The view inside might not be familiar, but it seemed triter than truth, nothing unexpected. Likely, every small-town police department had a similar long counter, a range of battered gray desks, linoleum that was always going to look scuffed. The place smelled vaguely of disinfectant and perspiration.

"Yeah, honey, what do you need?" The uniformed woman behind the counter had amazingly bleached hair, old eyes, and a printed tag that read *Martha*. Even though she looked buried in paperwork to the gills, she took the time to offer Lily a patient smile.

"Hello. I...well, I don't know who the sheriff is now, but I was hoping to talk to whoever may have replaced Herman Conner—"

"Chief Conner's right here, honey, nobody's likely to replace him until he gets around to retiring...which he said he was gonna do five years ago and still hasn't. *Chief*," she hollered, "pretty lady's here to see you."

"I've tole you and tole you, not to shout like I'm working for you. You buzz the phone or you come here to get m—"

Lily never expected to recognize him—and heaven knew, he'd aged—but one look and she was transported back in time. The sheriff probably never noticed her that night, but her memories were mirror-clear.

She and her sisters had been huddled on the curb; someone had dropped a scratchy blanket over all of them, but still they all shook. The sheriff's face had been backlit by fire as he was talking to the firemen. The sirens, the heat, the cold, the fear, the smoke—Lily remembered every taste, sound, texture. She wished she didn't. Her sisters had been mute like her, in shock like her. Cate, the oldest, had an arm tucked around Lily. Sophie, the youngest, was crying her heart out.

And Lily couldn't stop looking at the sheriff's face, because she'd identified him as the one adult who could give them some hope. Herman Conner was skinny as a blade back then—sharp nose, sharp bones, a fast, sharp decision-maker—some said impulsive. Some said, once he judged you on the wrong side, he never forgot. Everybody said he could make a body jump when he got riled up.

That long-ago night she'd kept fiercely trying to hear, kept hoping he'd make everyone jump this time. She wanted him to get her mom and dad out of that fire. She wanted him to do what sheriffs do. Make things better. Make them right.

Instead, he pulled one fireman aside—closer to the girls by accident; he was trying to get away from that madhouse noise near the fire truck. "Look," he said. "I don't see a reason to run too deep an investigation—"

"There's a lot of damage. A lot of—" Lily could see the fireman answering, arguing, looking unhappy, but she couldn't hear most of the conversation. The sheriff's voice had been closer and clearer.

"I know. I see. But we all know Campbell lost his job. Been what you call despondent. Three girls to support, no money coming in. I know he'd never have done nothing to hurt his family by intention. But I can believe a fire intended to get some insurance money got out of control."

"Herman, I agree that that's possible." The old fireman pulled off his helmet, wiped a river of sweat from his brow. "But unless we investigate, I won't have a clue how that fire started."

"There's only one likely reason. That's all I'm saying. And I don't want to hurt those girls more they're already hurt. You hear me? There'll be a cloud over their father's reputation as it is. You want to make that worse?"

"No, 'course I don't…."

Lily couldn't remember much else, but looking at Herman Conner now brought back that night, like being slapped with the heat and the loss all over again.

He might be twenty years older, but he was still tall and lean, still just as sharp-edged. He'd lost half his hair, and the eyes looked baggy and tired. When he barged out of the office and caught sight of her, his face turned pale under his ruddy tan.

"Sheriff Conner..." She stepped forward. "You have no reason to remember me, but I'm Lily—"

"Lily Campbell. And of course I remember you. You were the middle one with the big eyes. Never thought I'd see any of you girls in this town again."

Her polite smile froze. She remembered Pecan Valley as everyone being kind, with a lot of "honeys" and "ma'ams" and "bless her hearts" in drawling, liquid voices. Herman's tone wasn't harsh, just stiffer than starch.

"I wondered if you could spare me a few minutes," she said.

"Why sure. Got a mighty busy morning, but I'd always spare the time for a pretty girl, bless your heart, honey."

There was the old-fashioned Southern flattery she remembered; yet somehow, she felt increasingly uneasy as he motioned her into his office. *Office* was a nomenclature. The room had waist-high walls, with windows on three sides facing the central, open space. No private conversation was possible here. Herman hitched his belt and then plunked down behind his battle-scarred desk when she took the only spare seat.

She came immediately to the point. "I wonder if you still have the investigation record of the fire when my parents died."

"Aw, honey. I was afraid you were here for something like that. Sweetheart, it's foolishness. Your daddy was a good man. When the mill closed, he just lost his way, sank into whatcha call a depression, a serious depression. He adored you girls, you must know that. And your mama. He would never have done anything to hurt you, not deliberately."

"I believe that, too," she said. "But I'd still like to see the report from the fire."

"Well, the investigation report is public. I'm sure you know that. But I think it's a bad idea for you to go digging there, honey. There's nothing to gain. Nothing to know. We all knew what happened. Your daddy was desperate. Didn't know how he was going to support you girls and your mama. There wasn't a job to be had for quite a while, after the mill closed. What we think—what we all believed at the time—was that he set a fire for the insurance money. Only, he just didn't know much about accelerants, didn't know how or when such a fire could get out of hand." The sheriff leaned back as if relaxed for the first time all day. "We all felt bad. The whole town. And he died trying to save you girls, you know."

"I know." For an instant, the memory gripped her, the heat and choking smoke, her dad carrying each of the girls. The second-story drop. The firemen below. They were getting hoses and ladders and such, but that was all too late. She was the last one out the window, unwilling to let go of her dad, unwilling to leave him.

Then the drop into the dark night, the hard thump into the fireman's arms, and then...

Her dad silhouetted with the fire behind him—then the sudden woosh of fire and her dad disappearing, her screaming and screaming for him....

"There, there, little honey." Herman Conner lunged out of his chair, yanked a generic tissue from the box on his desk. "You need to forget about this all. It was a tragedy. An awful, awful thing. Hurt the whole town, too. But it just won't help to dwell on it."

"I've tried to believe that. But I've come to believe the only way I can move past it is for me to see those records for myself."

"Well, I'll see what we can scare up for you, of course. Where are you staying?"

"Louella's Bed-and-Breakfast."

"For how long?"

She couldn't stay more than eight weeks, not without risking her teaching contract for the coming year. But the answer she gave the sheriff was the one she wanted to be true. "As long as it takes."

He sighed. "All right. Well, I'll get Martha on it, and whatever we can chase up in the way of records, we'll send over to Louella's soon as we can. But my advice to you is, amble around town for a bit, remember the good times from when you three girls were little. If you're looking for what they call closure, that's the real stuff that matters. Remembering how folks cared about you all, your family, you three girls. Remembering what a nice town this was to grow up in, how loved you were.

Everything that matters, honey, it shouldn't be about that one unfortunate night."

"Thank you for the advice. And I appreciate your getting those records to me."

Lily walked out of the police station with her stomach a-jangle and her mind all tangled up. In principle, she knew the sheriff was right. Her sisters had managed to move on, find great guys, get over the past just fine. She *should* be able to do the same thing. She loved her job, teaching ultra-bright, challenging kids; loved her apartment in a historic part of Virginia, had many friends and things she loved to do.

But something inside her just couldn't rest. A lot of it was about her dad. She never believed he'd started that fire. Every memory of her dad was wonderful and loving, including the very last one, when he sacrificed his own life to save hers. He was no coward…yet that's what they'd always said. That he'd set the fire for insurance money, the act of a coward if ever there was one.

Her dad was a hero, not a coward.

She knew it in her heart.

She just had to find some impossible way to prove it.

Chapter 2

Two nights later, Griff heard the rare sound of fire engine sirens, followed by a rush of cop cars down Main Street. It was just nine, the sun thinking about dropping and the air drowsy with heat.

He was just shutting down the place. Jason had stuck with him, was pretending to do extra clean-up while Griff hunched over a table with the day's receipts. The day'd been busy. Everybody stopped for ice-cream on a summer day. Even so, the ice cream parlor couldn't support a cat, so it occasionally amazed Griff that folks actually believed he had no other source of income.

Of course, it had always worked well for him to be seen as a generic lazy scoundrel and a womanizer. Nobody pried any deeper. Why would they?

"You hear the sirens?" Jason asked.

"Yeah. First time all summer."

Jason squirted more window cleaner on the glass counter, even though he'd cleaned it twice already. "I heard some say they were worried about her coming back. That the fires'd start again."

"Say what? Who's this 'her'?" Griff looked up, only half-listening. He wanted to get out of here, put his feet up, open a dripping-cold long neck and start in on his real work. But the kid had been scrubbing the place until he'd practically worn out his hands; obviously he didn't want to go home. Bruises hadn't healed up from the last time his dad had a snootful.

"You know. The pretty lady who came in the other day. The one with the long brown hair. You went right over to her. Don't tell me you didn't notice."

Griff scowled. Sometimes the kid saw way more than he needed to.

Lily had been in twice more for Griff's Secret—but not for any of his. She'd chatted up Steve the first time; someone had talked to her the other. God knew, he'd raced from the back room to flirt her up, but she'd escaped before he could tackle her both times. Maybe that was accidental—or maybe she didn't remotely feel the same spark he did.

No sweat, he'd told himself. But somehow she kept pouncing into his mind, lingering there like a sweet taste he couldn't get out of his head. That he could get hung up on a woman he barely knew was downright worrisome.

It implied a capacity for commitment.

That was fearful.

Still, he couldn't let Jason's comment go. "Why would

anyone think that Lily Campbell has anything to do with the sirens?"

Jason rolled his eyes. "Come on. Her coming back after all these years just stirred up the story. Everyone knows what happened."

"Well I don't, so why don't you enlighten me?"

"Her daddy was a fire setter. That's what everybody said. And now she's back, so people been saying, 'watch out for fires.' And now you heard the sirens."

"That's pretty darned ridiculous, Jason."

"Hey, I wasn't even born when it all happened. I'm just telling you what people are saying, that's all. Her dad and her mom got burned up in the last fire. The three sisters, they got split up all over the country. People said the three girls, they cried and screamed when folks tried to separate them. That it all was a tragedy. That nobody guessed there was something so broken in Mr. Campbell. That was her daddy. Mr. Campbell. Anyway. The fires stopped after they left. Only now she's back. And there's a siren."

Griff frowned. "Jason, that's ludicrous. Who's spreading these rumors?"

"I dunno. Hey, don't be mad at me. I was just telling you what I heard, that's all."

"Well, think about it. If she left town when she was a little girl, there's no reason to think anyone even recognizes her. And if her father was an arsonist, that has nothing to do with her."

"I never said he was an ars'nist. I said he started fires."

"Jason. An arsonist is someone who sets fires."

"Sheesh. It's summertime. You're not supposed to have to learn stuff in the summertime. It's not fair."

There were times Griff loved living in a small town. This wasn't one of them. That young, pretty woman was soft clear through. It was in her eyes, her face, the look of her. That anyone could think she was a criminal—or in town for no good—was beyond absurd.

But Pecan Valley did love its gossip. And good news was boring. The chance of something naughty and meaty was always the ideal, but it was only now that Griff remembered—Lily had mentioned something in that short first conversation. Something about how he might not want to get to know her. He wasn't sure what it meant at the time. Didn't matter then. All he'd been concentrating on at the time was the lap of her soft tongue on Griff's Secret.

He'd imagined her tongue on a few other secret places of his in the days since, making him worry that he was turning into a dirty old man—before he was even in his prime.

"Jason."

"Yup?"

"You cleaned up enough. I'm locking up. I know you don't want to go home."

"Sure I do. You think I want to work all the time?" he said under his breath, "But you'll keep half my pay still, right?"

"Yup. Got it hidden. Earning interest." This was old, touchy territory for the boy. "I'm just saying. You find trouble at home, you know where I live."

"I'm not leaving my mom."

That voice. So low. So defeated. So old. "I never said you should leave your mom. I said you know where I live. Just like your mom knows there's a shelter where she'll be safe, and they'd help her start over."

"She won't go."

"That's not on you."

"Right."

Griff told himself to shut up, because he knew better than to push. He'd pushed before. He had four kids working for him—all troublemakers, school flunk-outs, all of them tattooed and pierced and familiar with the holding cell at the sheriff's office. You don't push kids who've already given up. And when a kid had already given up by age eleven, you tiptoed, because you might only have one chance to earn some trust—and that's if you were lucky.

Griff wasn't a good tiptoer. He wore a size-14 shoe.

Once Jason finally headed out, Griff thoughtfully packed up a pint-size cold tote and carried it to his car in the alley. Main Street was shutting down.

Shops closed up early on a weekday, but the pharmacy was still open and Deb's Diner still had a cluster of pickups in front. Although there was no sign of the fire trucks now, all the lights were blazing at the sheriff's office.

He noticed the lights, but didn't linger, just turned left two blocks later on Magnolia. The street was an antebellum postcard; the houses were huge and old, built of cool cinder block, most with sweeping verandas and swings hung with chains. Big old oaks shaded the sidewalks, but everybody had flowers, cottage roses under trellises where there was a peek of sun, bosomy peonies in the deep shade…he didn't know all the flower names. A fat fox squirrel chased right in front of his car—the measure of a safe town, he'd always thought, was that the darned squirrels knew perfectly well they had right of way.

The rich didn't hang in the neighborhood anymore, mostly because no one was all that rich—but the big old houses still looked loved, porches swept, gardens fussed over. Young couples who wanted a passel of children could afford the mortgages. The elders had already paid off theirs. Those in between had invariably turned their place into the ever-hopeful bed-and-breakfasts.

He parked, climbed out, took his tote. In the way of a small town, he knew Louella's even if he'd never been inside. It was the last on the block, with a red tile roof and long, long steps leading to the porch…he didn't initially see her. At least not exactly. What he saw from the rail on the veranda, were a pair of very bare, very dirty, very feminine feet.

Judging from the position of those feet, they were attached to someone who was lying flat on the wood plank veranda floor. A curious position for sure.

He ambled up the sidewalk, up the steps, to peek his head over the rail.

The glow of lights and distant voices murmured from beyond the B and B's giant screen door, but the only one on the veranda was her.

For a moment, his heart stopped—he wasn't sure she was alive. She was lying there with her feet up on the rail, eyes closed, arms just lying at her sides, palms up…

as if she'd fallen in that kind of heap and couldn't move. She was wearing shorts and a tee in some pastel color, all wrinkled and tangled.

His heart immediately resumed beating on noting she wasn't wearing a bra. And that her plump, perfectly shaped breasts were rising and falling, indicating life— not to mention a delectably appealing rack.

By the time he'd finished a complete study—legs were damned good, way, way better than he expected, a little Yankee white, but the calf shape was just that perfect arch of a curve. Anyway. By the time he finished, she had one eye open.

"Please," she said. "Go on in. Leave me for dead. There are all kinds of people in the house. If you want someone, just pound on the door."

"I was looking for you, actually."

"No point. I'm useless. In a state of complete decline. I can't move, can't talk, don't even care anymore."

"Are we…" he tried to think of a delicate way to phrase it "…having a little trouble adjusting to the heat?"

She closed the eye. "There's air-conditioning. That's what the ad said. It didn't lie. I bought a thermometer yesterday. My room's cooled off to eighty-seven degrees. Now go away. I can't stand anyone watching me while I sweat."

"I brought ice cream."

"Beg your pardon?" One eye slid open, then the other.

"Griff's Secret. A pint. Two spoons. Cold."

"Say it again."

"Ice cream."

Silence. Then… "I don't know why you went to the trouble of tracking me down, but I absolutely don't care. You can have whatever you want. Just show me the ice cream."

He lifted the pint container.

She swung around to a sitting position faster than a jet takeoff. "Spoon," she said.

He produced two from his polo shirt pocket—as well as a hunk of napkins.

"Do not watch me eat this," she instructed. "I intend to inhale. And I may drool. You need to understand. Thomas Wolff had it right: 'You can't go home again.' I'm hot. I'm miserable. No one likes me. If I were you, I'd hide behind the veranda rail. Protect yourself from being seen with me."

If she made love with half the enthusiasm that she ate ice cream, bless her heart, Griff might just have to propose. Of course, he'd have to test that theory. And at the moment, she definitely didn't look *in the mood*.

When he didn't interrupt her ice cream inhaling to intrude with conversation, she piped up. "Did you hear the fire truck siren a couple hours ago?"

"Yup."

"I set that fire."

"Did you now?" He didn't lean over to clean up the dab of Griff's Secret on her cheek, but man, he wanted to.

"I'm not sure what street it was on. Or where it was. In fact, I didn't have any idea I'd set the fire until an old busybody four doors down came storming into Louella's kitchen to track me down. So, if that's why you stopped

by—to hear it from the horse's mouth, so to speak—
now you've got it direct from me. The fire was all my
fault. I did it. Fire setting's in my blood. I'm nothing but
trouble. The only reason I came back to town was to
cause trouble."

"Thanks for sharing." Okay. He couldn't stop himself.
That bit of ice cream on her chin was too tempting to
ignore. Her eyes shot to his when she felt the touch of
his finger. His eyes shot clear-cut communication right
back.

So. He didn't have to worry anymore that she didn't
feel the same electric click that he did. Both of them
knew—speaking of fire—that there were potentially
explosive sparks.

"I took one look at you," he said, "and before I had a
clue about all that history, I just knew, right off that bat,
that you were a wicked, wicked woman."

"Watch it. A compliment like that could bring tears
to my eyes. Most men who first meet me seem to
immediately figure out I'm a pretty plain old ordinary
schoolteacher."

"Plain old ordinary? That never crossed my mind. I
took one look and thought there's a breath of fresh air
in this town. A gorgeous, sexy woman, who can make a
T-shirt look like designer clothes, has eyes a man could
drown in, with character and mystery surrounding her
like magic."

She almost choked on the last spoonful of ice cream.
"All right, all right. You know I've been here a couple
days, so as you might have guessed, I already know your
story. You charm every female that's ever crossed your

path—whether they're two or ninety, married or single. You've gotten a marriage proposal from every single woman in a three-county radius—"

"Not every single one," he corrected.

"Just most. And I can see why. You're adorable and all."

"Thanks."

"You started out in Savannah. Hard to imagine why you'd settle in this itsy-bitsy town. But lots of people have been happy to fill me in on why they think you came here—even if I never asked. And I really don't need to pry into your life or anyone else's."

"I understand. Once you're inside the town limits, it hits like a wave. The hot air from people talking about each other. There's no escaping it."

"Who knew? Anyway…let's see what else I was told. You can, of course, correct or deny any of this. You come from a good family—that means, a *Southern* family, a family that was established here long enough to fight in the War of Northern Aggression. You went to a good school, North Carolina, I think I was told. Played B-ball. Everybody remembers that you graduated, but not what field you graduated in. No one's sure if you ever had a real job. Somehow, you didn't feel like making anything special of yourself."

"That's me. Just lazy as can be."

"Yup. That's how I heard it. Thankfully, you invented and patented your own ice cream. Maybe moved here because the cost of living was extra-reasonable. You can sit around all day and just make a little ice cream, hire kids to help you, and spend the rest of your time romancing all the pretty Southern Belles. Why should everyone need to be ambitious? Why should you do hard work if you don't have to? Only…none of the girls have caught you. In bed, maybe. In affairs, maybe. But nobody's caught you anywhere near the altar, or that's the story I heard."

"Anything else?"

"Anything you want to deny so far?"

"Oh, no," he assured her. "Gossips have the story absolutely straight."

"They usually do," she said without missing a beat, and finally turned her head to face him. "So I might ask you what your real story is. Sometime. If it's something you're interested in sharing."

"I was going to make the same offer. To listen if you needed an ear."

She turned quiet, the devilment in her eyes fading. A moment ticked by, then another. The bustling noises inside the house had faded into the single noise from a television. Lamplights had turned on throughout the neighborhood.

The sun had taken its lazy Southern time going down, but it finally ebbed out of sight, nothing left but a deep violet haze beyond the trees and rooftops.

He didn't realize how much time had passed, how late it had become…but it seemed as if she suddenly did. "You know what?" she said.

"What?"

"I'm glad you stopped. You didn't need to. It was beyond kind—particularly for a man who seems to have a mighty reputation in this town for not caring much about others. You keep that kind streak really well hidden, I gather."

"I'm not kind." Sheesh. It was like being accused of larceny or something. No guy liked to think of himself as *kind*.

"It's okay," she said. "I won't tell. I just brought it up because I didn't want you to think I needed looking after. I knew coming back here would be tough. I'm all right." Rather than leave it on a heavy note, she came through with a grin and added, "Except, of course, for dying of the heat."

She uncurled her legs and started to clean up the spoons and ice-cream container. Griff didn't need a bat over the head. It was time for him to go.

Heaven knew what sparked the impulse to visit to begin with. The buzz of gossip coming from Jason had just nagged on him. The sound of the fire truck siren had annoyed him further. He just kept getting some stupid, uneasy feeling that Lily was alone in town and in trouble.

So—fine. He'd come and brought her ice cream and they'd made each other laugh. Everything was great. Time to pack it up. Hell, he'd lost a couple hours of the real work he did at night as it was.

Yet they both stood up at the same time. He reached for the container at the same time she extended a hand to offer it. She was still smiling at him, friendly fashion. She'd absolved him of any responsibility. She was tough, she'd implied. Prepared for trouble, she'd implied. No one needed to worry about her, she'd implied.

This close, for that millisecond, he saw a pearl of

perspiration on her neck. Saw the tilt of her head, proud, stubborn. Saw the sunset in her hair.

He had to bend down almost a foot to kiss her. Didn't know he was going to do it. He didn't plan it, and didn't intend to. He was holding the sticky spoons and container, so it was a no-hands kind of kiss, couldn't be any more, couldn't turn into more.

Yet her face tilted to accommodate the landing of his mouth, not as if she was inviting him, but as if she just instinctively moved to make a meeting of lips more natural, more easy. He tasted ice cream. He tasted the vulnerable satin of her lips.

He lifted his head almost immediately, saw the startled flush on her cheeks, thought…oh yeah, she's tough, all right.

Tough as a rose petal.

"I'll give you a discount on ice cream if you show up regular while you're here."

"As if that was an offer I could refuse." But her eyes shied from his now. The sass was still there, the ready teasing…but she didn't know what to make of that kiss.

As he ambled down the walk, headed home, he thought, hell times ten, neither did he.

Chapter 3

Lily had serious things to think about—why fires had started up in Pecan Valley since she'd shown up, the facts surrounding that long-ago fire, whether there was a chance of finding more information that might clear her dad's name…and, oh yeah, that extraordinary kiss from Griff the night before.

The man had been humming in her dreams all last night. But this morning she couldn't concentrate on anything because of her landlady.

Louella Bertram was eighty if she was a day, never met a cat she didn't like, made coffee so weak it looked like dirty water, and treated every guest as if they were skinny runts that she took in just to feed.

"Now, sugar." When Lily tried to rise from the breakfast table, Louella was already trying to block the doorway. "You can't go a whole day on a sip of coffee and a half a bite of toast. You'll waste away in the heat. Now you just take a little bag along with you. It's just a couple of my cinnamon muffins, something to tide you over. You end up here at lunch, you just come on back to the kitchen, and I'm sure I can whip up something for you."

She'd been here less than a week, yet Lily already knew better than to argue. She took the bag, then, when Louella lifted her wrinkled cheek, bent down to give her a smooch and a hug. Louella wouldn't let her out the door without those, too.

"Now," the older woman walked her to the door, "I know you think you want answers to the past. Everybody wants answers. The whole South, we understand about how the past and our history is part of who we are. But sugar, the things that matter in life, you never find those kinds of answers in facts. It's all in the heart. So I'm not saying you shouldn't look, honey. But I just want you to enjoy being back in your home town, instead of dwelling on that one bad moment. Your momma and daddy had a good life here once. You try and think about that, child."

"Yes, ma'am."

"And another thing…"

Lily escaped inside of ten minutes, the best she'd managed to do so far. Carrying her purse and a satchel— and the muffins—she headed straight for the street. She didn't have a thermometer, but outside, this early, it couldn't be more than one hundred and ten. In the house, it was hot enough to fry eggs.

She'd given up jeans in the first two days, then gave

up skirts, and that was the end of her traditional teacher clothes. Her shorts were barely decent, her tee tissue thin, and if this relentless heat didn't let up, she planned to walk around naked with no apology. She'd neglected to get her long hair lopped off, but that was only because she'd been too busy to check out the local salons.

Two blocks later, she paused at Griff's place. Naturally, this early in the morning it was still locked up. She didn't expect to see him. It just seemed to be a knee-jerk reaction—walk by the ice cream place, remember that kiss. Remember his sitting on the veranda, feeding her Griff's Secret, making her think about other seductive secrets he might offer.

To the right woman.

Under the right circumstances.

He was a player, she reminded herself. A womanizer. An uncommitted, lazy, adorable scoundrel. There wasn't a soul in the town who'd suggested anything else.

Truthfully, it was his lazy scoundrel persona that rang her bells. It had been so long since a man rang her bells that she couldn't believe it. Somehow, though, she couldn't manage to believe his reputation. Something was...off. He kissed like trouble. He looked at a woman like trouble. She didn't doubt that he *was* trouble.

But a sixth sense still warned her that he was not what he seemed.

Like everything else in this town.

Another block later, she opened the door to the police station, which had become as familiar as Louella's. The same Martinet Martha guarded the front counter, gave her the same two-second acknowledgment, then barked,

"Chief, someone to see you!" at the top of her impressive vocal range, same as before.

And Herman Conner, after a few moments, clomped out of his office, hitching up his trousers, with the same refrain. "How many times do I havta tell you—" And then he spotted her. Sighed.

"You gonna visit me every day this week?"

"Not every day. But I just—"

"Come on in, come on in."

"You're busy." Phones were ringing. Printers clacking.

"Not too busy for you, sweet thing. We need to get your mind satisfied so you could finally put all this to rest." He motioned to the same scarred-up wood chair he had before. "I'm having coffee. You gonna be here long enough to have a mug?"

"I could kill for a cup."

He sighed again. "Not a thing to tell the sheriff, honey."

She propped a peace offering on his desk. "Cinnamon muffins. Fresh."

He opened it, smelled. "All right. I admit it. There is good in you." She got the coffee. He got the muffins. She opened up the satchel and pulled out her faded copy of the police report.

"Not this again," he said.

"I just have a few more questions." She leaned over the desk with her copy of the investigation report. It was only three pages, and that included signatures and dates and times and addresses. The actual information related to the investigation was sparse—which was why she'd read and reread it until her eyes crossed. "At the very end of the report, you wrote, 'no reason to connect this to the other arson fires'. That kept jumping out at me. *What* other arson fires?"

"You've been on the computer again, haven't you? That, or watching *Law and Order* reruns. Everybody's an expert on the law these days."

"I'm sorry to be such a pain," she said, real apology in her voice, but not moving until she'd heard an answer. He sighed and eventually got around to responding.

"You know, it's been twenty years, but if I recall correctly, there'd been a rash of vandalism fires, stretching maybe a year or so, before the one at your place. But there was no relationship, like I wrote. There was no one killed in the other fires, no property damage that remotely compared."

"Still, was there *any* similarity with my family's fire? Like…was the same accelerant used? Or were those fires set in the same time of day? Any connection at all?"

"The similarity you need to know, sunshine, is that the arsons stopped after your daddy died. For a whole three years, there was no other fire except for old Samuel Wilson's trying to cook after his wife died. So this is probably not an avenue you want to pursue. It only points to your daddy all over again."

That hurt. She admitted it. Still, she said softly, "So you're sure…there was no similarity in the other fires?"

"To be honest with you, sweetheart, I don't remember now. I just remember studying the thing at the time, concluding there was nothing in common with the other prank-type fires. If you're doubting I know how to do my job—"

"No, no." She hurried to look penitent…and to push the other cinnamon muffin his way. Being a teacher, she had a half-dozen ways of locally researching the past fire, all of which she still intended to pursue—but there'd be no real way to get closure without Sheriff Conner on her side. If she had to grovel, she was more than willing to grovel. "I'm just trying to understand, sheriff. It was so devastating to my family—"

"And to everyone in this town. Now—you got any more questions?"

"Just one teensy one." She motioned to the partial sentence on the second page. "The report says the fire started outside our back door. Actually, it says, west of the back door."

"Okay. And you think that means *what?*" the sheriff asked with a look of fatherly patience.

"Well, I'm not sure. But I *remember* our house. We shared a garage wall with the house next to us. And that my dad had a shop on that side of the garage. He liked working with wood, so he had stuff out there, like lacquer and varnish and mineral spirits and all that."

"I'm still listening."

"Well…I had no concept when I was a little kid, but now, it seems pretty obvious why the whole downstairs exploded. Why the fire was so fast and awful. Because of the chemicals my dad had in the garage."

Herman Conner took the last bite of muffin. "Okay."

"But my dad would never have deliberately started a

fire near those products, would he? That wouldn't have made any sense at all. The belief was that he wanted the insurance money. But he loved us. I can't imagine in a million years why he would have started a fire where all those accelerants were around. It would have been asking for an explosion. And he'd never have done anything to deliberately harm my sisters or my mom—"

"Lily. Honey. We've been over this. He was despondent. He'd lost his job. He wasn't thinking rationally."

"But isn't it possible…that the fire might have started in the house next to ours? But that ours went up so fast because of the stuff my dad had in the garage? I mean, do you know who lived next door? What happened to them? I don't remember at all—if that house burned down, too, or if anyone was hurt there, or anything else. If there could have been a connection…" Lily could have sworn she caught a flash of alarm in the sheriff's eyes, yet his voice was as calm and patient as before.

"Aw, sweetheart. You got eyes full of hope. But there was no one in that house. It'd been for sale for several months. There was fire damage there, too, a course, but nothing like what happened to your place, where the downstairs fire took off like hell in a fury. Pardon my French. You were all trapped on the second floor. There was no one on the other side of the garage wall to be hurt."

"So. You think that's a dead end," she said carefully.

Something had changed in his expression. His posture was a little stiffer, his eyes more guarded. Or maybe it was her imagination, because his tone of voice never changed.

"I think, if you want to come back here every single day you're here, ask more questions, pursue anything on your mind, honey, then that's what you should do. Let's get this off your mind so it'll never come up again. I admit, if I were your daddy, I'd be advising you to let it go, that it's not good for you to dwell on something you can never make right. A tragedy is a tragedy, honey. You already went through it. No point that I can see in reliving it yet again. But you do whatever you need to do. I won't get mad. That's a promise." He added, "Particularly if you keep bringing me Louella's cinnamon muffins."

When Lily left the station, the temperature had risen to one hundred and thirty—at *least*. Virginia had hot summers, but nothing like this. She battled the humidity straight to the ice-cream store—which, she told herself, had nothing to do with seeing Griff. It was about saving her life.

The place was wallpapered with kids, some slurping ice cream, but not all. Lily recognized the phenomenon. With school out for the summer, the kids too young for a job needed a hang-out place. Griff's was clearly it.

Two boys were manning the counter, with a third visible in the back, doing washup. Griff seemed to choose employees who looked as if they'd recently been let out of juvenile detention—lots of tattoos, lots of metal on their faces, lots of attitude. The one Lily had come to know—Jason—seemed to half-live there.

"You looking for Griff?" he asked when she made it up to the counter.

"Well. It doesn't look as if he's here—"

"He's here. He's just locked up."

"Locked up?"

Jason nodded his head toward a far steel door. "He's in the vault. It's where he makes the ice cream. Nobody's ever allowed in the vault, but I can let him know you're here—"

Before Jason finished the comment, Griff appeared from beyond the locked steel door. As if expecting her, he turned and located her in two seconds flat. That slick, wild kiss on the dark veranda was suddenly between them as if it just happened.

Possibly, she'd have had the good sense to run out the door, if he hadn't crossed the room too quickly for her to take that option.

"I don't want to interrupt you," she said immediately.

"You won't if you come back with me. I'm right in the middle of something."

"Jason just said no one's allowed back there?"

"No one is," he agreed, and motioned for her to follow him.

All right, all right, so she had more curiosity than could kill any cat. After a word with his kids, Griff led her into the so-called vault. "You can test one of the new flavors I'm experimenting with," he said.

She tasted. Then tasted again. The flavor had some peach, some pecan, some vanilla bean, some unique and tantalizing other flavor. She took another spoonful, thinking that when she left this darned town, she was going to be fatter than a pig.

Which didn't stop her from more taste testing, even as she turned in a slow circle, examining his "vault."

The room was long, clean as a new penny, all stainless steel and bright light. A one-way window supervised the shop—so that was how Griff knew exactly what was going on with the customers and kids—and inside were counters and a bunch of futuristic appliances she couldn't identify. Ice-cream making equipment, obviously. She would have asked a dozen questions, except that Griff clearly *was* in the middle of something, had put on gloves, had some kind of quietly vibrating blender that he was supervising—so he got in his grilling first. "How'd your visit with the sheriff go?"

"Pretty much the same as the other times. I raised questions. He called me a fool. I thanked him." She gave him more rave reviews for the new flavor, but he still had questions.

"Where are you going after this?"

"I figured either the newspaper office or the library. Wherever I can dig into old copies of newspapers the easiest. I assume old editions will be available online—"

"Maybe not online. But likely on microfiche."

"What's microfiche?"

He chuckled. "Spoken like a Yankee. We just don't do technology at the same rate you northerners do, sugar."

"Hey. Virginia isn't north."

"It is, compared to a small town in Georgia."

"But I was born here. Don't I get credit for being true Southern?"

"With those legs, in those short shorts, you can get all the credit you want."

She didn't think he'd noticed. "Speaking of which…"

"Speaking of your legs, or of credit?"

"Credit. You've been giving me a lot of free ice cream. I was thinking I should go the same path as the other women in town and fall at your feet."

His eyebrows lifted. "I like your thinking."

"So…I'm asking you to dinner." Actually, Lily had no intention of walking in here and making that suggestion, but now that it was out, she was going with it.

"Hmm. I'm guessing you've been stuck with restaurant food since you got here. So how about dinner at my place?"

"That'd be okay—but it doesn't solve the problem of my being in debt to you."

"I don't need to solve that problem. I love women in debt to me."

She rolled her eyes. "Your place. But *I* cook—to erase the ice-cream debt."

"This is sounding complicated. On the other hand, I like complicated. How about if I pick you up from Louella's around five. We can grocery and wine shop together. Then go back to my place and sip something tall and lazy while you cook."

"A reasonably good plan," she said, "except for not knowing where you live."

"Close enough for you to walk home if I come on too strong, sugar."

Several hours later, Lily was just starting to seriously consider that question. It seemed unlikely that Griff would actually come on at all—much less, come on too strong. Yeah, there'd been those kisses on the dark veranda, but maybe she'd built those up in her mind. Unlike her sisters, she'd never attracted a hot kind of guy. Good men, yes. Gentle guys, decent guys with all the important boy scout qualities—but never scoundrels.

At least other women seemed one hundred percent certain that he was.

As they wandered around the local grocery store, she picked out chicken breasts, fresh parmesan, bread crumbs and aimed for fresh potatoes next. Lily wondered if it was possible to make it five feet without yet *another* woman flashing a smile at Griff. The smiles all had the same brand—the kind of slow, Southern smiles that told a man he was the best thing she'd ever seen in a month of Sundays.

By the time she caught up with him the next time, she'd gotten the potatoes—and everything else she'd sent him after—and found him cornered between the oranges and grapefruit by a redhead in frayed denim. He spotted Lily. His eyes lit up—not necessarily out of exuberant lust—since it looked as if he'd have groveled to anyone who could save him from the buxom redhead's gregarious chatter.

"Lily! Mary Belle Johnson…this is Lily, Lily Campbell."

The redhead whirled around, green eyes narrowed—took in Lily in a glance. Instead of spitting fire, the woman's face immediately calmed. Possibly, it was Lily's simple blue crocheted top and white capris that conveyed that she was just no competition for Griff's attention. Not compared to a woman with Mary Belle's substantial figure and charming ways.

"I swear, Lily, I been hearing about you since you got into town. My daddy told me you'd come back. I was wondering if I'd have a chance to set eyes on you." The woman lifted a critical hand to her hair. "I could do something with that."

"You—?"

"Yeah. I run the salon on Main Street. Belle Hair. I do makeovers, too." Another evaluative look at Lily's face. "I really know my eye makeup." Mary Belle glanced down at her hands. "And manicures."

"Well, thank you so much." Lily didn't laugh, but she was inclined to. She hadn't been insulted so thoroughly—or so kindly—since she could remember.

Griff took off with the grocery cart toward the checkout like a bat out of hell. "That's the scariest woman in town," he said sotto voce, when Lily finally escaped and caught up with him.

"Come on. You could handle her with both hands behind your back."

"Are you kidding? I was about to dive into the grapefruit. See if a commotion might make her go away." Griff shot her a wry look. "She didn't seem to upset you. And as far as I could tell, she was trying her best."

"I desperately need a haircut. And a woman knows never—*ever*—to offend anyone who could have power over her hair."

He let out a husky chuckle. "You *don't* need a haircut. It's great the way it is."

"Why thank you, sir. But you don't have to waste flirting on me."

"Waste? Since when is flirting a waste?" He paid for the groceries, scooped up both bags.

"I saw what you were doing. The blonde. The second blonde. The brunette. Then the redhead."

"What? What?"

"You were telling the ladies that I was with you. Which'll be all over town—" she glanced at her watch "—probably within the next ten minutes. Is that why you asked me out to dinner? To make sure people knew I had a friend in town?"

"Are you kidding? I have no interest whatsoever in being your *friend.*"

Man, he was full of the devil. It was good for her feminine ego. But his protective streak—no matter how vociferously he denied it—was as transparent as glass. "She mentioned her daddy—"

"Yeah. The sheriff. She's Herman Conner's daughter."

"I thought you said her last name was Johnson?"

"I did, but it's darned hard to keep track. Mary Belle's changed her last name around three times in the last decade. She must have been about ten years older than you back then. The wildest thing this town had ever seen. Gave her dad gray hair and then some. Drank, smoked funny stuff, partied and stayed out all night. No one could put a rein on that girl. Or that's the story."

She'd forgotten—or maybe she'd never known—how much fun it was to get caught up in the soap operas in a small town.

The groceries fit snugly in the back of his red convertible EOS. The car suited him. It was seriously green, but it was also splashy and sassy and high tech. Not a gas guzzler, yet still perfect for a guy who wanted a sexy scoundrel's image. "So why do I keep getting the impression," she asked, "that you're not quite the lazy bad boy you let on?"

"You're such a breath of fresh air. It's been a while anyone believed I had a serious bone in my entire body." He shot her a glance. "Mostly because I don't." As if to prove his point, he gunned the baby. Of course, even driving at breakneck speeds, his place wasn't more than a couple miles from town center—so it wasn't as if he kept up that life-threatening pace for long. As he'd said, she could walk home later if she was so inclined or needed to.

His place wasn't what she'd expected. Of course, she hadn't expected anything in particular. But his land was so close to town, and yet nothing like town. Just off the highway, he turned onto an unmarked road, sneaked up past a sea of lodge pines, into a burst of sunshine, and finally there it was, a house perched on a rock ledge, the same color as the native pale limestone.

All the rolling hills in their Georgia neck of the woods made finding a hideaway easy enough, but Griff had made his place so…invisible. Almost as invisible as the dirt-crusted, practical pickup truck parked behind on the garage, on a slab of concrete in the shade.

"Like it so far?" he asked, not referring to the pickup—which he couldn't realize she'd noticed—but to the facade of the house.

A half hour later she was dredging chicken into a whipped egg, then rolling each piece in a batter of fresh parmesan. Griff had opened a bottle of something red and dry, poured it into a couple of fat glasses, and for a laid-back kind of guy, was jogging circles around her.

He'd already made dessert—yet another new flavor of ice cream he wanted her to try. He'd also pulled out hors d'oeuvres from the fridge, plump white shrimp on ice, with a sauce so spicy it could turn a nun hot. His eating table was beveled glass, with thin teak slabs for placemats, already decked out with sterling flatware and water goblets.

The view from the counter where she was forking the chicken into a frying pan, was of a mountain. The entire east wall was glass, overlooking a secret dark forest below, where occasionally she could glimpse a sterling ribbon of stream.

"You know, I didn't really expect you to cook." He kept circling, leaning over her shoulder. "What *are* you making?"

"You'll love it. Trust me."

"How do you know?"

"You're male." She grinned, took a sip of wine, then scrounged in his cupboards for the extras she needed. Aluminum foil. Spices. A good olive oil.

He'd never exhibited a trace of nerves before—at least not around her. Yet temporarily, he couldn't stand still or relax. Lily thought she knew why. She was discovering, whether he wanted her to or not, that Griff was a class-A liar.

His general decorating scheme was minimalist to the nth degree, but that was misleading. He'd built the place to be a private hideaway, which it was; but the design, constructed right into the hillside, had to cost a fortune. The inside surfaces were all expensive, from hardwood to marble and limestone. The bathroom off the main living area was done up in lapis—the real lapis—and the shower itself had one glass wall overlooking the mountainside.

A deer could do the voyeur thing, for heaven's sake; the man must have no modesty at all. And since Lily'd had to use the facility, she'd accidentally noticed his office, because it was right across the hall. These days, everybody had their computer corner, someplace where dusty cords reproduced on the floor and a desk was heaped with paper. But not like this. Griff's office looked something like a war room at the Pentagon. She had no idea what work he did—particularly since he claimed to do no work at all beyond experimenting with ice cream for fun—but that office was no play station.

She wasn't quite sure how she wanted to deal with the liar yet, so she focused on the immediate priorities. Once the browned chicken was popped in the oven, she tested the potatoes. They were almost ready to mash. She searched for a bowl, then collected sour cream, cream cheese, fresh chives, shredded cheddar and pepper.

"Your kitchen's beyond awesome. Is this where you play with the ice-cream flavors?"

"Almost never. The vault at the store is ideal for working with that."

"There's nothing more ideal than this kitchen that I've ever seen." She finished another sip of wine, then added, "Be ready in about ten."

"I set up right here." He motioned to the glass table.

"But that doesn't mean we have to stick to that plan. If you want to eat outside—"

"Bite your tongue, handsome. I can see that gorgeous patio outside, but it's okay with me if I never experience heat again."

"You're a wuss, Lily."

"Tell me something I don't know."

He stopped talking altogether, once the food hit the table. It couldn't have been a more ordinary dinner: mashed potatoes, fresh asparagus, the chicken parmesan. She'd figured what to cook based on a single factor. He was a guy. So normally, he wouldn't take the time to make ordinary good food.

And from the way he was shoveling it in, she'd judged that question fairly well.

"Did I mention before that I was in love with you?" he asked.

"You didn't, but I was expecting it. I'm sure you say that to all the girls." She enjoyed the flirting. She still hadn't figured out why he was flirting with an ordinary schoolteacher—like herself. But it seemed pretty darn silly not to like it. Life was too darn stressful these days not to savor a smile when she could win one.

"Yeah, I do. But this time I mean it. Where'd you learn to cook like this? Would you live with me? Would you like jewelry, diamonds or rubies or something? Now's the time to ask," he assured her. "There's probably nothing I wouldn't give you."

"Oh, good." She finished eating long before he did. She poured him another glass of wine—she'd had enough—and cupped her chin in a palm. "I want to hear where you came from. How you ended up here."

"Aw. You don't want to hear that boring old history."

She raised her eyebrows. "You said I could have anything I wanted."

"Okay. You asked." He reeled off the stats. Core family based out of Savannah, but his father was career military, so there was a lot of moving around. He had two younger brothers, one living in Idaho, the other in Vermont. He'd gone to college.

She made a disgusted sound. "Okay. I take it you never want me to cook for you again?"

"Whoa. Wait."

She made a come-on motion with her hands. "Less bare bones. More real story."

The sky blurred, blued, backdropping the hilly landscape with jewel colors and softness. When he talked her into going outside on the slab of a white patio—and it took some convincing—she discovered it wasn't hot, not this high above the tree level. Instead, it was cool and serenely peaceful.

She sank into the cushioned lounger next to him, and accepted a bowl of his newest experiment. It was some kind of mix of blueberry and cherry and mint. Tangy. Sweet, but provocatively so. Different.

Like him.

"MIT is not a generic 'went to college'," she informed him. "You should have *said* MIT before. Then I'd have known you had a scary kind of mathematical brain and I'd never have come to dinner."

"You can't just tell people you came out of school a mathematician. They don't know what to do with you. What do you think of the flavor?"

She took another spoonful. "I think it's outstanding. The one in the store this morning—that was good, but more universal, a flavor everyone could love. This one is in a class by itself. More refreshing than rich. Flavors that blend in ways you're not expecting. You're good at this."

"Yeah, I think so, too."

He made out like he was so full of himself, but Lily was beginning to see that was just more of his tomfoolery. And it seemed about time to let on that she wasn't that easily tomfooled. "So far, just for the record, you haven't told me a single thing that adds up. Your field's mathematics but you make ice cream. You started out in Savannah but your family seems to be all over the place. And where do women or wives or children fit in this picture?"

"I'm not good husband material. Which I realized a long time ago."

"Did you discover that by being a husband?"

"Man, are you nosy."

She got it out of him, but it took another glass of wine—for him, not her.

It probably helped that the sun dipped below the tree line, creating a concealing darkness and sense of privacy. Griff likely didn't realize he'd forgotten to use all his usual "honeys" and "sugars" and all that other flirting nonsense.

The man she discovered behind the protective layers

intrigued her—more than intrigued her. He clearly hated talking about himself. But what he grudgingly revealed exposed…well, Lily wasn't sure what to call it. Depth. Heart. A man deeper than a well.

"My father was old-line, straight military. He wanted the family to run like a machine. You obeyed him right now, no asking questions, no excuses. I was the oldest."

"So it was worse for you." It was all too easy for Lily to read between the unsaid words.

"I'm not saying it was worse. Just that being oldest made things different for me. I didn't want him raining hell on my little brothers. They cowered from him as it was."

He didn't say his father punched him regularly. Lily didn't ask. But she could see the blank expression in his eyes. Hear his light tone.

"When I turned eighteen, he wanted me to sign on for the military. I wanted to go to college. We had a fight. A serious fight. It was the first time I ever hit him back. He had me arrested, thought that would be a good lesson for me, and told me that I'd see what it was like to spend the night in jail, see if I felt like disrespecting him ever again."

Lily stopped breathing. She was afraid if she said anything, she'd cry. For him. For the pictures he was putting in her mind.

"You have to understand—my dad thought he was raising us with love. He just thought boys needed to be tough to survive, to 'be men'. He thought toughness was a sign of character." His gaze narrowed. "That's the fourth glass of wine you poured me, Lily. You trying to get me drunk so you can have your way with me?"

"No. Finish the story. How'd you end up at MIT?"

"A seriously decent scholarship. A lot of work. A lot of debt. I see my mother every few months, call her more than that. But I don't see him. My one brother turned out just like him, a bully all the way. The youngest brother called me when I was at MIT. Johnny was in the hospital, broken collarbone, broken wrist. I came to get him. I was in no financial shape to take on a kid brother—particularly when my father took me to court. But we managed okay. You heard enough?"

Again his voice was lazy and teasing, as seductive as the moonlight.

She answered as she had the last time. "No. It's still a long way from there to owning an ice cream parlor in Pecan Valley."

"Actually, it's not that far. I made certain decisions, once I was grown and had my kid brother on his feet. I was never doing anything requiring discipline as long as I lived. That includes wearing ties, relationships and any kind of work that takes effort."

"Griff?"

"Yes, honey."

"You are *so* full of baloney."

"What I *am* is embarrassed. I can't remember the last time I told this story, probably because I never did. I was raised with better manners than to bore a charming, beautiful woman. We're wasting this moonlight. I never— it's the cardinal rule of my life—waste moonlight."

For a man who'd had four glasses of wine, he was out

of the lounge chair faster than magic. His eyes met hers in the darkness as he coaxed her out of the chair, pulled her close, pulled her into him.

Okay, she told herself. *Okay.* She'd been charged up from the first instant she met him, and she knew it. He was full of baloney, he charmed her, enticed her. Made her want to experience—just once!—being involved with a bad boy, a man who knew his way around women, who just plain *liked* women and knew what to do with them.

Every woman she knew had flings. Why on earth shouldn't she?

She realized she wasn't experienced in being wild and loose, but she was willing to practice. He was ideal to take lessons from.

It was just…the more she knew him, the less she believed of his bull.

And now he'd completely messed up the fantasy. Kissing him wasn't about the wild, loose, immoral fling she'd had in mind. She liked the damn man. He was lonely, a solo flyer. Tons of people claimed to "love him", but no one she'd seen so far actually seemed to *know* him. Much less *really* love him.

Not like a person needed to be loved.

So really, it was entirely his fault that it all just got out of hand.

He swooped her in his arms, and even though she wasn't exactly sure how to seduce a seducer, she swooped right back.

Chapter 4

Griff couldn't fathom how she'd so completely messed with his head. Kissing her was supposed to be about... well, about kissing. One of the most enjoyable activities in the universe. A prelude to an even more enjoyable activity.

And a side benefit of kissing her was shutting her up—not that Griff was thinking in such crass terms, but hell and a half, she'd somehow gotten him talking about personal history. He never did that, and never wanted to do that. Hell, he never even allowed himself to think about the past. The whole point of burying something was making sure it was nowhere near the surface.

Her scent, on the other hand, was dangerously near the surface. He was falling into this drug, this unexpected intoxicant made up of all the textures of Lily Campbell— her scent, her taste, her thick lustrous hair, the butter softness of her lips, the sweetness of her. The latter was the killer ingredient. He just wasn't prepared for that yielding sweetness, the way she tipped her head back, the way she leaned into him, to him.

Hell times ten. What *was* it about this woman? His arms swept around her, wrapping her closer, as if to protect her from the moonlight, from chills and dangers that didn't exist, from…him. She was a teacher, for heavens sake, not a Lorelei. She gave off more nerves than an untried girl. She wasn't a player.

Every Southern girl emerged from the womb knowing how to flirt, knowing the danger line, enjoying the sport. Not Lily. She drifted off when he tried to charm her. And now, when he expected her to bolt because he was crossing the danger line, she curled around him as if inviting Armageddon. Hoping for it. Daring him to bring it on.

Hands skimmed down her sides, testing, exploring. Beneath her thin top, he could feel the suppleness of her skin, the warmth. The allure. Her eyes closed against the impossible brightness of moonlight. She sank into his touch, into yet another kiss, not yielding so much as communicating yearning.

Slow, wary of scaring her, rushing her, of doing anything to break this crazy spell, he eased the side of his hand against her breast, heard her responsive intake of breath, felt the heat rush straight to his groin. His arousal was no surprise, but he was hard to the point of pain, hard like a teenage boy who could only think of one thing.

Having her.

Dipping deep into that softness and heat.

He brought her closer, achingly close, burning close, his hands sweeping down to her fanny, pressing. Her breasts crushed against his chest, nipples tight, igniting another firestorm of hunger, of awareness, of want.

Responsively, she swayed even more snugly against him, shimmying just a little against his arousal, nestling against it. At that precise second he understood she was saying yes. That he could have her naked, have her in his bed this night. All night.

Even more confounding, he couldn't remember wanting a woman more.

Ever.

That thought was enough to scare a little sense into him—not a lot, but enough. He eased back from a kiss, pressed his forehead to hers, tried to remember how to breathe normally. Since they were still glued hip to hip, possibly, normal breathing was highly unlikely, but maybe he didn't want that much sanity quite yet.

"What are we doing here?" he murmured, knowing exactly what they were doing. That was the problem—an intense awareness of how right, how damned perfect, she felt in his arms.

"You don't know?" she whispered back. "I could have sworn you started this."

He hadn't. He'd started a kiss, yes. He'd intended to thoroughly enjoy a devastating, thorough, evocative good-night kiss. But she was the one who'd brought on the tsunami, not him.

"You've been seducing me," he accused her.

"Trust me. It had to be you doing the seducing. I wouldn't know how to begin."

"Oh yeah, you do." Her nonsense made him smile. Or maybe it was that hypnotic look in her eyes. He swayed against her, wanting to, needing to torture himself a little longer. "We're going to make love aren't we, Lily Campbell…."

"Is that a question or a statement?"

"Oh, it's a statement for damned sure. But not tonight." He heard the landline ringing in the house.

So did she. She straightened. "You need to answer that."

"Yeah, I do. But I want you to know, if it weren't for a potential emergency call, I'd let it ring until ten months from Tuesday. It's not about wanting to stop this."

"Griff." It rang two more times while he tried to explain. "Just go. It's all right."

It wasn't remotely all right. He could barely walk straight, and his head was still buzzing. But he always answered the landline phone at night. He only gave the unlisted number to so many people—like his boys. Jason and Steve were in the riskiest situations at the moment.

He grabbed the kitchen extension, prepared for…hell, prepared for anything. He'd had to be in the past.

Instead of a boy's voice, though, he heard the gruff tone of Cashner Warden, the fire chief. "Griff. Got a fire at your shop. The fire truck's on its way, but I'm driving in from home as well."

He saw Lily pausing in the doorway, then her expression changed to immediate concern. She'd obviously grasped that something was wrong.

"Was anyone in the store? Do you know how bad the fire is?"

"Not sure of anything yet. Neighbor saw smoke, called nine-one-one. I know you got a sprinkler set up in there, so I'm hoping that—well, it's foolish to speculate until we know more. I'm on my way."

"I'll be there." Before Griff could hang up, Cashner got in one more question.

"Griff. You happen to know where Lily Campbell is?"

Griff frowned. "Say what?"

"I'm just asking. If it's arson, my first thought would normally be one of those loser kids you take on—but that's not so logical, considering you're the one always bailing 'em out of trouble. So then I have to say. You know. It's the second fire since she's been in town."

"That's ridiculous," Griff snapped, and hung up.

"What?" Lily asked. "Something's wrong—"

"Fire. At my ice-cream place. I have to go."

"Of course you do. How can I help?"

He couldn't remember the last time anyone had offered to help him. And his first response was to say the male thing—"of course not." Yet, even before he'd grabbed a light jacket from the hall closet, he'd rethought that. "Something's wrong, Lily," he said quietly.

"Obviously. A fire's a terrible—"

"Not that. Or not *just* that. I'm not sure if you heard, but the fire last week was at the old mill. The place is deserted these days. Nothing to worry about, as far as damages. Someone just brought in a heap of trash and lit a match to it. But it happened to be…"

There was a sudden stillness in her face. "Yes. Where my dad used to work. Where he lost his job. That's why, of course, *I* set that fire."

It was as if she'd turned inward, to a place he couldn't see, couldn't be. He heard the joke. He just understood that it wasn't really funny—not to her—and damned if it was for him either. "Yeah. First thing the fire chief asked me was whether I knew where you were."

She took in a breath. "Wow. So I set this fire, too?"

"Amazing, isn't it? Really, sugar, I already realized you were amazing. But I had no idea you could be two places at once."

"Some women have that kind of magic." She was still joking, even though her face had turned pale.

"I don't like this." He couldn't define why adrenaline was shooting so fast through his veins, but every protective instinct was charged on full. Two fires in less than two weeks. Lily's name publically associated with both of them. What was going on?

"I can't seem to think straight," he admitted. "My first instinct is to suggest you come with me, be with me, so people will see us together. I'd think that would prove you aren't the fire setter. Unfortunately, the plan's full of holes. I could be stuck at the shop for an unknown stretch of hours. Makes no sense to strand you without a car."

"This is easy, Griff. I'll drive with you. I'd like to help if I can. And if there's nothing I can do, then I'll just walk home to Louella's."

He was about to object. He liked her plan—except

for letting her walk home in the dark. Just then, though, they both heard the distant scream of the fire truck.

There was no time to argue about logistics or details. She even beat him to the car.

In every way, Lily wanted to help Griff, to step up and do whatever she could. She'd just kind of forgotten a couple things.

Like that she was petrified of fire.

Like that she tended to have panic attacks anywhere near serious smoke and flames.

The instant Griff turned on Main Street, the chaotic scene flashed in front of them. Griff stiffened as if someone had slapped him—then moved. He pulled the car over, didn't waste time parking it, just cut the engine, tossed Lily the keys, opened the door and took off running.

Lily climbed out quickly, too, but then couldn't seem to move. The fire truck couldn't have been there long, but firemen manned two hoses, both of which were aimed full-force at the ice-cream shop. People clustered as close as they dared, some in their nightclothes, some holding kids and crying. The hoses choked the sharp yellow flames, turning everything into a black, sooty mess. The crowd, held back by yellow tape, screamed when the front window of the shop blew out, raining shattered glass glittering onto the wet pavement.

Griff was still charging under the police barrier toward his store.

Lily struggled to unfreeze. She knew this nightmare, every sharp edge, every petrifying shadow. No one knew about the furious noise of fire unless they'd endured it. No one knew about the choking smoke, the impossible mess, the stink. No one knew how something beautiful and safe and sure could be devastated in mere minutes.

No one knew that you could lose everything that ever mattered to you faster than the snap of two fingers.

She shook herself, forced herself to breathe, to move. This wasn't about her. It was about a whole town—and Griff losing that treasure of an ice-cream parlor. In the distance, she saw both the sheriff and fire chief jog over to reason with him, talk with him. Images nailed in her mind. Griff, fighting to get to his store, scalping a hand through his hair when he was held back. Sheriff Conner shaking his head. The fire chief, Cashner Warden, cocking a foot forward, clearly asking question after question. Griff never took his eyes off the fire.

Lily scanned the crowd, trying to think of something, anything she could do to help. The townspeople all seemed to love Griff. There wasn't a kid or family who didn't stop for his ice cream, barely a woman who didn't take the time to flirt with him. Several kids in the crowd were crying, hands to their mouths, being comforted by moms and dads whose faces looked white in the darkness. Every few moments someone would look at her—including Sheriff Conner.

It hurt to see suspicion in their eyes. They unquestionably thought the fire was caused by arson.

Darn it, so did she.

She spotted two of the boys who worked for Griff— Jason and Steve—and instinctively walked toward them. In such a relentlessly clean-cut town, the boys stood out like weeds in a garden. They were huddled on their own, isolated from the crowd, both wearing tees too thin for the damp night, shoulders hunched.

The tall one, Steve, had arms decorated with tattoos and his hair dyed with a stripe of red. But for all the belligerent expression, he had the eyes of a lonely kid.

The other boy, Jason, was scrapper-small, his head shaved like a marine's. He'd saddened Lily from the first time she met him. He had that beaten look in his eyes, a posture that was always anxious, spring-ready—ready to run, ready to punch, ready always to face the next bad thing.

Both boys recognized her, saw her walking, but neither paid any attention until she stopped in front of them. "Hi, guys. Have either of you been here long enough to know what happened?"

Jason looked behind him, as if thinking she must be speaking to someone else. When he realized she was talking to him, his face flushed.

"He got here first." He lifted his shoulder toward Steve. "But I got here right after. We both wanted to help, but the cops and firemen won't let us go any closer."

"But we're not leaving," Steve said. "We're staying for Griff. No matter what anybody says."

"That's exactly how I feel," Lily told them. "I don't want to leave if there's a chance I can help. But to tell you the truth, I'm really petrified of fires. Would you mind if I hang with you two?"

Both boys shot each other a look of alarm. Yet they both immediately moved to create a space between them, then promptly looked around as if expecting someone to explain the facts of life to Lily. There were respectable people all over the place that she could be talking to.

"Did you hear anything about how the fire started?" she asked.

"Lot of people talking, but nobody who knows." Steve shifted on his feet. "It wasn't, like, electrical. Because it wasn't in the walls or like that. And the one fireman, he was talking about accelerants. Like how fast a fire burns, how it burns? I heard him say something about gasoline. Which means somebody set it."

"Nobody shoulda done that to Griff," Jason said heatedly. "Nobody."

"That's exactly how I feel," Lily agreed. "I don't know him well. But as far as I can tell, he's decent to everyone, not at all the kind of person to make enemies. More like the kind of man who'd make serious friends."

Steve lost some of his stiffness. "He doesn't care who you are or where you come from. You're good to him, he's good to you. He doesn't rush to judge people."

"That's my impression, too. So, can either of you think of someone who might have done this?"

Jason toed an imaginary spot on the cement. "Some people think that'd be you. Not that I'd be thinking that, of course. But some people been saying that."

Steve shot him a look. "Not *us*. Griff, he set us straight about you. We know you're okay."

Lily kept an intrusive eye on Jason's face. "I can't tell you how much I appreciate hearing that. It really hurts to have people think the worst of you—especially when they don't really know anything about you."

Jason suddenly squinted at her hard, then said slowly. "Yeah. I know what that's like."

A moment later he shifted a little closer. She knew better than to push for any closer connection this soon. The gifted kids Lily taught tended to be well dressed and quiet, wealthy kids; but these two were so similar in other ways. Her students all had sharp edges, radiated the same don't-fit-in loneliness. They were always braced for people to judge them as "different."

In the meantime, the crowd was slowly drifting away. The smoke was still thick, the burned stench pervasive, but the fire was out, the danger clearly over. The fire truck had turned off its flashers. The authorities still hovered with Griff. Lily was uncertain how much time had passed. One hour? More? For darn sure, it was well past midnight…and the two boys were weaving on their feet.

She didn't ask if their parents knew where they were. She would have bet the bank it was a waste of time. She just said, "I can see they're starting to close this down. And I was thinking…"

"What?" Steve asked.

"Well. Nobody's going to be allowed to touch anything until they take off the yellow tape—which I assume will be tomorrow, at the soonest. But the thing is—it really looks like a mess."

"You're not kidding," Jason said.

"Griff is really going to need some help. But not now. So, it'd seem the best thing to do for us is to go home and get some rest. Because he'll need all the energy we've got to help him tackle this tomorrow."

"I don't think we should go," Steve said.

"I know. It feels wrong. But I keep thinking, if we're all exhausted tomorrow, how much help can we really be for him? And there isn't a prayer anyone will let us do anything tonight."

"I don't know," Jason said unhappily.

But twenty minutes later, when the last bystanders disappeared into the night, the boys finally agreed to pack it up—after some more ardent words about being there for Griff first thing the next day.

Eventually, the fire truck left. Then the sheriff drove off with the fire chief right behind him.

An older man with a thatch of gray hair parked in front of the place, opened his windows—it looked as if he'd been assigned to stay the night, make sure no one trespassed on the fire scene until morning. Griff stood talking with him for a while after that, before turning around and aiming for his car.

Initially, he didn't notice Lily sitting on the curb, which suited her just fine. He wasn't devil-may-care womanizer Griff now. The lazy stride was gone.

He was mad. He had to be beyond exhausted, but he stalked toward the car with a clipped step, an iron cast to his chin, his mind obviously working overtime at a hundred miles an hour. The character in his face fascinated her. So did the splotches of soot decorating his clothes and arms and face.

He was startled when he suddenly spotted her. "What are you still doing here, you crazy woman?"

"I figured I'd take you home." She stood up, wiped the cement crumbs from her fanny.

"I assumed you'd have already gone home. You weren't supposed to wait—"

"I wanted to." She wanted to wrap her arms around him right then, too, but she didn't. He moved tighter than wire, every muscle coiled up and bunched. "It was arson, yes? Gasoline as the accelerant?"

"Yeah. I take it you heard some of the talk." He scraped a hand through his hair, which only added more soot to the mess. "It's actually not as bad as it looks. The clean-up will be a godawful mess, for sure. But the two locked rooms in back—the freezer section, and my experimental kitchen—those would have taken serious money to replace, and they're fine. It's just the main part of the store that's a wreck. Apparently, someone used a skeleton key, dropped a homemade gasoline explosive in a wastebasket. It seems impossible. A crime with no motive. Vandalism for no purpose. But planned."

"So..."

"So, the fire team needs to see the scene by light of day. Do their investigative thing. Then I can get in there. Rather than clean up, frankly I suspect it'll be easier to gut the place, start with new sheet rock, new floor, just redo the darned thing. What?" He seemed to suddenly notice that she was dangling her car keys in front of him.

"I want to hear more," she assured him. "But it's been a long night. Let's get you in the car first. I'll take you home."

"You're taking *me* home?"

"Don't get your hopes up. I'm not offering a wild night of sin and surprises. You're just not going home alone tonight. I'm driving, because you have to be stressed. Then I'm putting you in a hot shower, and after that, tucking you into bed."

He shot her a look. "I don't think so," he said dryly.

She did.

She was gaining a certain comfort level in this odd, powerful attraction she had for him. It was like looking at a diamond so expensive that she couldn't have it. Griff was a fantastic flirt, but he couldn't *really* be interested in her. His home was here. Hers would never be here again. He played a sophisticated game. She went to makeup and jewelry parties. He had a secret life. She never had a reason to keep a secret. Bottom line was that she might as well let this singing, zinging fire between them smoke through its course, because she couldn't imagine how she could get burned. He wasn't for her. She'd never lie to herself about that.

But tonight wasn't about such heavy issues. Tonight was just about watching over a man who was beside himself and worn out.

His house was dark. Neither had thought to leave an outside light on. Griff gave her grief every step of the way, insisting she go home, that he didn't need a babysitter, that he could get his own towels—when she turned on the shower, she prowled around for a linen closet and clean towels, then prowled in the kitchen until she found a bottle of Talisker's.

She wasn't exactly positive what kind of liquor that was, but when she unscrewed the top and smelled, she knew it was exactly what she was looking for. She splashed a couple shots in a water glass, and put that on the bathroom counter, too.

"If you're determined to stay here, you could at least come into the shower with me," he called from the other side of the smoky glass.

"Maybe next week," she said.

"What? What's next week?"

"The point is that you're not getting any tonight, so just get your mind off it." She left the door ajar, and went into his bedroom. The master suite wasn't particularly huge, but the balcony was a pool of moonlight, the room colors a rich blend of silvers and pale grays and charcoals. She plumped his pillows, turned back the sheets.

She debated what to do with the clothes he'd peeled off—her first choice was to trash them, but really, she hardly had that right. The fire stench was too noxious for them to stay inside, so they got a temporary home in his garage.

Griff emerged from the shower still protesting—but his voice was starting to slur, his eyes bloodshot from all the smoke. She pointed with a royal finger—her teacher royal finger—toward his room. "I'm not tired," he said. "And besides that…"

She didn't need to tune him out. He was out for the count from the instant his head hit the pillow. Actually, he crashed so deeply that she was a little fearful he'd gone straight into a coma—but his chest was rising and falling, so there was no excuse to keep hovering over him.

Because she couldn't find any herbal tea, she poured

herself a thimbleful of that Talisker stuff, found a blanket from his linen closet, and curled up in an oversized chair in his living room. With that location, she was within springing distance of his landline, just in case anyone dared try to call and interrupt his sleep again.

She expected to nap, but couldn't. She was too troubled—by the fire, by why arson fires had suddenly started when she came back. By why anyone would target Griff. By that long-ago fire and the memory of her dad's face in the window, backlit by flames....

Unsettled by the old nightmares, she scrounged in her purse for her cell, thinking that maybe it was past time to consult with the big guns. She used to either call or email her sisters several times a week—but that was before they'd both fallen in love last year. Their guys were great, but her sisters had been so insufferably, relentlessly happy that they couldn't talk about anything but *her* finding someone. Tonight, though, she just plain needed sis time.

Because it was the middle of the night in D.C., she couldn't call her youngest sister, Sophie. But Cate was honeymooning in Alaska, and the time there was relatively early evening.

"You are in *such* trouble." Cate not only immediately answered the phone, but started right in with the bossy business. "You haven't answered your email in days. Sophie said she hadn't heard from you either. What's going on?"

"Guilt," Lily admitted. "I knew you'd yell at me if I told you what I was up to."

"Of course I'm going to yell at you." Cate adjusted

the phone, said something to Harm—her good-looking groom—informing him that a girl had priorities. Sex was an important second. But sisters came first. "Now— where are you? And I don't want to hear that you're spending your whole teacher summer doing stupid stuff like jewelry parties and gardening and volunteering endless hours for some godforsaken cause. I want to hear that you're up to no good. With a man. Preferably a bad boy kind of man. Preferably—"

"Yup," Lily said peaceably. "I'm doing exactly that."

The silence between Alaska and Georgia was abruptly deafening.

"What?"

"For years now, you two have been urging me to strip off the teacher clothes, quit being nice, quit dating safe guys. So I took your advice—"

Cate, in a crisis, didn't fool around. She cut through the drivel. "Where are you? I can get the next plane out."

Lily smiled into the receiver, but then got serious. "I'm in Pecan Valley, Cate. I'm looking into our fire. Or trying to. I know we've talked about this a zillion times, that we need to put the fire behind us, take charge of our lives. Only you and Sophie have done that. And somehow I haven't been able to."

"Wait. Honey. Wait. If we knew you wanted to do this—or needed to do this—the three of us could have found some time to come together, go there together—"

"No. You'd both have tried to talk me out of it." Lily

snuggled up tighter in the blanket, leaned her head back. "I never thought Dad started that fire. We all repeated the things we were told. That he loved us, but he was desperate, not in his right mind—all that. But I never believed it, Cate. Every time I'm with a guy...I'm thinking of dad. How much I loved him. How perfect we all thought he was. How good. And that if he set that fire, maybe I can't judge *anyone's* character. Maybe I'd just love blindly. Trust blindly. I'm probably not explaining this well, but—"

"You are, Lily. But I hate the idea of you doing this alone. And what about this man you mentioned?"

Lily heard her brother-in-law's voice in the background, and figured she'd interrupted enough. "Cate, I'll talk to you in another couple days, promise. Don't worry. Everything's fine. Give Harm a big hug from me. Love you."

She switched off her cell, thinking she'd prowl around Griff's place one last time, make sure all the doors were locked, make sure he was sleeping, make one more run to the bathroom.

That was the plan. But the last thing she remembered was snuggling just a moment longer in the blanket. It wasn't as good as Griff's arms around her, but thinking about Griff set off a chain reaction of dreams.

Chapter 5

Griff awoke with his heart pounding, the threatening smell and heat of fire invading nightmare after nightmare. Immediately, of course, he was fine. His bedroom was familiar, dark and cool and safe. And his bed damned lonely.

He vaguely remembered Lily bossing him around, bullying him into the shower, absconding with his clothes, ordering him into bed. He couldn't recall ever being so offended...male-ego offended. The bossiness had charmed him. But then, she didn't even seem to notice when he was naked in the shower, and later tucked the covers around his neck as if he were a boy instead of the sexiest man she'd ever seen in her life.

It was enough—almost—to destroy a guy's confidence.

The bedside digital claimed it was 3:00 a.m. He'd only

slept two hours, was still groggy with exhaustion. Still, he pushed off the covers, swung his feet to the floor. First thing in the morning, he needed to devote 100% effort to the fire and all the fire's complications. But right now there wasn't a prayer he could get any further rest without knowing where Lily was.

She could have gone home of course, just taken his car. That would have been a no-sweat. And when he checked the spare bedroom, the couches, and didn't find her, he thought she'd had the brains to do that—but no. The bunched-up blanket in his favorite recliner had a body swallowed in it. He had no idea how she'd managed to curl herself into that small a ball—much less how she'd escaped being smothered.

When he peeled back the edge of the blanket, he found the gleam of her dark hair in the moonlight. But she didn't awaken. He scooped her up, blanket and all. That didn't awaken her either. Her cheek nuzzled against his shoulder, as if she'd been sleeping against him her whole life.

Halfway through the hall, he almost tripped because part of the blanket slipped, tangled with his bare foot. But he managed to compensate, pushed against a wall—none of that commotion woke her either—and finally made it to the bed.

He dropped her on his side, his pillow, and when the last of the blanket slipped away, realized she was still wearing clothes. He hesitated. This wasn't about seduction, it was about…something else. Showing her that he didn't need taking care of. Showing her that he could take care of *her*. Or something like that. Still,

sleeping in clothes seemed bulky and uncomfortable.
So he pulled off her knee-length shorts—or pants—or
whatever they were. Then he re-covered her, and finally
sank onto the other side of the bed, and discovered the
strangest thing.

His body went bone hard the minute his skin touched
hers—that was neither a surprise nor remotely strange.
But somehow, just the act of wrapping his arms around
her, her just being there with him, felt crazily, insanely
right. In spite of the fire and all the troubling questions
threatened by that attack of arson, he was able to
forget it, really close his eyes this time, and zone out
completely.

Lily woke to the soak of sunlight on her closed eyelids,
her body all cuddled in a nest-warm cocoon—and the
erotic, rhythmic stroke of a thumb on her shoulder.

A man's thumb.

Her eyes popped open. In her immediate vision was
a bunched-up blanket, a shoe twice her size, a shirt she
could have used for a tent and a wide window overlooking
a steep, green hillside. Only strips of sunlight made it
through the tangled thatch of trees, but the verdant spice
of pine scented everything. A bird suddenly landed on
the windowsill—gorgeous, bright blue in color, an indigo
bunting, she was pretty sure. It cocked its head, looked
at her as if to say, "what on earth are you doing in his
bed, you crazy woman?"

And still, that thumb kept stroking.

She knew perfectly well where she was. Griff's. But
she could have sworn she'd fallen asleep in his living

room chair. A thousand unexpected sensations all seemed to require her immediate analysis. His bristly chest hair against her back. The weight of his hand. The width of his hips, spooning against her bottom. The hardness of his erection. The size of his erection. The throbbing warmth of his erection.

She strongly suspected that she wasn't the only one awake. Not that she was willing to turn around and face him yet.

"I have to think up a strategy," she murmured, and he picked it up as if they were in the middle of a conversation.

"For how you're going to go back to the B and B?"

"Exactly. If I were back in Virginia, it wouldn't matter. I'm an adult. Everyone around me is adult. But here... Louella's going to grill me as if I were ten years old, the instant I walk in the door. Being absent for a night is one thing, but if I also walk in wearing yesterday's clothes..." She lifted the sheet. "Uh-oh. I seem to be to be missing some of yesterday's clothes. Something happened to my capris."

"I was helping you." Griff's voice was still husky with sleep.

"Uh-huh. I'll bet you say that to all the girls."

"Lily."

"Hmm?"

"I don't say that to all the girls. In fact, there's a giant list of things that I plan to say and do with you. That I've never considered doing with anyone else."

Talk about a way to melt a girl. Griff's Secret, she thought, wasn't just an ice-cream flavor. It was this ingredient in him, a secret, insidious factor, that annihilated defenses and seduced a heart without half-trying. She turned in his arms, well aware they were suddenly breast to chest, tummy to tummy, danger zone teasingly rubbing against danger zone.

"Hey," she murmured worriedly. "Where's that kind of talk coming from?"

"I don't know," he admitted. "But you're scaring me. I barely know you."

"That's supposed to be my line. I'm the girl, re-member? I'm the one at risk if I fall in love with a guy who's reported to have no settle-down or responsible genes in his entire DNA."

"That's me," he admitted. "If I were you, I wouldn't get involved with me either. I've never had a committed relationship in my life. Never bought a ring or shopped for one. Never had the energy or ambition to."

Oh, for Pete's sake. He'd been selling that snake oil since she met him. Being only a pinch away made it easy enough to...well, to shut him up. It was as simple as laying her lips against his.

On his.

With his.

Yearning shot through her bloodstream like a silky streak of surprise, crazy strong, achey wild. He tasted so good. He tasted like everything she'd been forbidden, everything she'd secretly dreamed of.

His tongue dove inside her mouth, combined tastes and textures, at the same time his knee eased between her legs. His hands swept her body—up, down, roaming, igniting the slope of her spine, her fanny, back up...

She twisted in his arms, not kissing him back—more—feeling inhaled. Taken in. Taken under. She'd liked kissing him before. She'd liked his touch. She'd liked that electric sensation of risk and desire, the rush of need and want. But this was different.

Recklessness. She'd never tasted it before. Heat. She'd never suffered from it before, not like this. She'd been afraid of fire her entire life—but somehow not with him.

Not this kind of fire.

She opened her eyes, saw his—dark, intent now, not playing. He looked at her as if she was the only woman he'd ever wanted, the only woman he'd ever needed. The hunger in his touch, his eyes, his mouth, was more than sexual. It was about loneliness. Gut loneliness. The kind where you knew there was no one else who could accept you, all of you, who could know you, all the way inside, and still want to be there.

She didn't do fantasies like that. Ever.

But with him... Her breath caught when his palm found her breast, cupped, then squeezed. Her hand slid down his side, down his bare hip, knuckled inside, to cup where he was hard and hot. She squeezed.

"Okay," he hissed. "You're in real trouble now."

His head disappeared under the covers. She didn't quite remember when she'd lost her shirt, but her bra was still on, all a tangle, straps around her arms, cups pushed away. He got rid of it altogether, started sampling slopes and valleys of skin, found freckles between her breasts, found each nipple, analyzed each thoroughly with his tongue—until she was gasping for breath, and her legs reflexively clenching. He roamed down her tummy, found her navel and appendix scar….

"Hey," she whispered. "Maybe…hold on there. Just for a second. Maybe…wait. Maybe I need to think about this."

"No."

"No? Huh? You can't say no. If you vote no, we stop. If I vote no, we stop. Those are the rules."

"Now, Lily, trust me. I know the rules. Come on, though. Give me a chance to be a hero. I'm in the striving class. Don't know what I'm doing. You could help me learn. You could give me an achievement badge if I'm good. Or a whack upside the head if I goof this up. See? No risk."

She almost laughed at his words. Only, Griff wasn't a fledgling, and he knew—awesomely, brilliantly, inventively—exactly what he was doing. *She* didn't. Oxygen locked in her lungs when he dipped lower, scooped her legs in his arms, and sampled tastes and textures with his whiskery cheek and his lips and his tongue.

She stopped thinking. Stopped breathing. Forgot her name. Forgot just about everything but that she was female, pure female, and Griff, damn him, was more man than she'd ever dreamed existed. She gulped in pleasure, greedily wanted more, needed more. Needed him. Yelped his name in her angriest tone, her bossy teacher tone. "*Now*, Griff, and quit fooling around—"

"Okay, okay, I'm coming up," he promised her—only right then his landline rang.

Then her cell phone did its bell tone thing.

And then his cell phone did some kind of jubilant chime.

The three noxious sounds struck her as a blast from planet Earth. For a little while—for an insane, wonderful, breathtaking little while—she'd forgotten about reality. Her fire. His fire. The way that past seemed to be strangely spilling over into the here and now.

Maybe she'd been haunted all her life by fire. But she'd never been afraid…until coming home again.

Now she tasted fear. And the upsetting flavor of guilt—because somehow, her history with fire had managed to hurt Griff.

"I got a proposition for you."

The only proposition Griff wanted was from Lily, but he turned around to face the new interruption. Debbie, from Debbie's Diner, had straw-dry, big blond hair, boobs so big you wondered why she didn't fall on her face just trying to walk and was decent to the core. She always chose the wrong men, made fried chicken so good it could make a rock salivate, never met a dog so ugly she wouldn't take in. She was one of the best commerce neighbors on Main Street.

She peered into the burned-out shell of Griff's ice-cream parlor and clucked in sympathy. "I was thinking, Griff, I got spare freezer space. We could put your ice creams on the menu in the diner until your own place is up and running again. That way, you could use up the ice cream so it's not wasted, and I'd get more customers coming into the diner just for the ice cream. We'd both win."

Debbie had barely left before Manuel Brook showed up, tapping him on the shoulder. Manuel came from a family of farm workers, and had gotten a business started cleaning carpets. He barely reached five-four, had beady little eyes, and a wife—some claimed—who regularly slapped him around. "Hey, Griff. You got a big mess here. I clean up fire and water messes before. Once you get the debris out, you call me. I'll do the cleaning, my own time, on me."

"That's not necessary." Griff said immediately, but it had been the same story all morning. Neighbors and friends stopped by, didn't waste time sympathizing, just dug straight in with offers of help.

Margo, his insurance agent, had been on the site almost the minute he'd parked the car. "I know there are still questions as far as the investigation goes," she told him. Margo was well over sixty, spare as a reed, hair the color of iron. "But I don't want you worried about the claim. I sold you good coverage, and I'll have a check to you as fast as we can get the details on paper and get it processed."

Every kid who'd ever worked for him showed up through the morning as well—the ones who'd been in jail, the ones who couldn't stop fighting, the ones who'd been drinking hard liquor since fourth grade. Not a clean-cut kid in the lot. Yet all of them showed up, offering to help, offering to shoot whoever did this, offering to stand guard, offering to hang with Griff in case anyone else tried to hurt him.

By noon, Griff couldn't keep his eyes off the street. He hadn't forgotten that wild body in bed with him this morning. For damn sure, he hadn't forgotten what had unfortunately been interrupted by the blast of phone calls. He also hadn't forgotten finding Lily sitting on the curb last night, waiting for him, hanging with his boys.

When they'd split this morning, she said that she was going back to the B and B, needed to shower, clean up, change clothes, and then she'd be here. It wasn't as if either of them had set a timetable.

He hadn't been worried about it—until the sheriff and fire chief had stopped by, taken him out back to have a quiet talk.

His fire hadn't been accidental. Maybe Griff had already guessed that, but it was still another thing to have "arson" put in indelible ink.

His fire had started from a gasoline accelerant, exactly like the accelerant used in the deserted mill fire the day after Lily arrived in town. Exactly the same accelerant had been used in that long-ago fire that took her parents' lives.

Gasoline was one of the most common accelerants arsonists used, the fire chief told him.

He got it.

But he'd never liked coincidences. And he didn't like not knowing where Lily was.

Damn town was full of the best people a man could ask for in neighbors—friends, people who cared.

But someone wasn't so nice. Two fires in less than two weeks? No record of arson in years, until Lily suddenly came back in town? It just didn't make sense.

Lily couldn't escape the B and B to save her life. As fast as she'd gotten here from Griff's, she'd tiptoed in the back door, scooted up the back stairs in bare feet, and hustled inside her room. Trying not to make a sound, she'd peeled off her clothes, grabbed a satchel of toiletries and opened the door to go into the bathroom.

And there was Louella, standing there with a heap of fluff-dried pink towels. "I thought you'd might appreciate some fresh towels, honey."

"Thank you so much."

"The whole town's talking about the fire at Griff's. And I worried when you didn't come in last night. But I told myself, Louella, it's none of your business. She's a grown woman, I told myself. But then I remembered, you don't have any parents to watch out for you, and you're young and pretty, and I don't like to—"

"Louella, I absolutely have to take a shower."

"Of course, you sweet thing. You just go on. I won't say another word."

And she didn't, she just turned around and headed for the stairs—yet somehow, her beaming face was there when Lily opened the bathroom door twenty minutes later. "I wanted to tell you that I'd saved you some cinnamon rolls from breakfast. But also, since you missed breakfast, I thought, well, you might like a little sandwich with me."

Lily had never lived with anyone so intrusive,

but Louella was like an honorary grandmother. An unshakeable honorary grandmother. She managed to pull on clam diggers and a violet cami, swooshed up her hair with combs—she *had* to get it cut or she was going to go out of her mind. Louella watched her apply brush, lipstick, mascara.

And since Lily still hadn't managed to shake her by then, she figured she might as well try grilling Louella. "Were you living here when the mill closed?"

"Of course I was. That mill closing almost killed the whole town."

"Did you happen to know my dad? My mom?"

"Of course, honey pie. Your mom—she thought the sun rose and set on her daughters. She always had you dressed so cute. And y'all had manners, not like kids are raised now. All you girls could shake a stranger's hand, say hello, sit quiet in church. You were angels, all three. Although I have to say, your older sister—"

"Cate."

"Yes, that one. She had a little hellion in her. Used to make me laugh. I can remember one time, your mama must have wanted her to have a bath—she was maybe four? And Cate, now, she didn't want it, ran out of the house stark naked with your mama chasing after her, carrying a baby under one arm, must have been you? And Cate, oh my…"

Lily wanted to laugh. She could easily picture her independent older sister being that kind of handful—but just then, she couldn't be diverted. "Louella, do you know if there are people still living here who were connected to the mill back then? Anyone who might have known my dad?"

By then, Lily had herded Louella down the stairs, through the kitchen, had accepted a wrapped bag of something homemade and fragrant—but before Lily could leave, Louella had parked her ample body in front of the screen door.

"Well, yes," she said slowly. "The owner of the mill back then was Webster Renbarker. Your daddy was his second in charge. The mill didn't close because it wasn't thriving, you know. The place did real well, once your dad took on the management reins. Everybody said so. The problem with Webster was that he got a brain tumor. Started acting goofy. Hid his own money from himself. Sabotaged his own shipments. Nobody could figure out what was going on until it was too late."

"He died," Lily assumed with a sinking heart.

"Oh, he's alive. It was just nothing at that point could keep the mill from bankruptcy, between Webster's shenanigans and his medical bills. Came a point, they took out the tumor. He lost the sight in one eye, as I recall. And he'll never be what you'd call normal. Lots of days he's fuzzy. That's what I hear from the grapevine, anyhow—"

"I don't suppose you know where he lives?"

"Why, sure I do. Lives in North Carolina, some place for seniors. Has some supervision. You know. That kind of place."

"Okay." For a few moments, Lily actually thought she had a real lead. She tried not to feel disappointed as she aimed firmly for the door. "Well, thanks for sharing all that, Louella—"

"A course, he's here now."

Lily whirled back. "Say what? You mean here? In Pecan Valley?"

"Well, yes, for a couple more days. He's visiting his wife's cousin, Barbara Marr, it's an annual thing they do in the summer, bring him here for a week, take him back. You know the Marr house, the red-tile roof at the far end of Magnolia Drive? He was here last week at least. Remember seeing him at Debbie's Diner. Not like he can't do some things on his own. He just tends to be unpredictable, bless his heart. And when he's home here, people look after him, not like anything was his fault. Right after…"

A minute later, Lily was gunning the engine of her rental Ford. If this Webster Renbarker was shortly leaving town, she had to try to reach him before the chance was gone. Griff was going to wonder where she was. She wanted to be with *him*, not gallivanting all over town on what was probably going to be a wild-goose chase.

But if there was even a small chance the long-ago fire had a connection to the immediate fires, she had to try.

She knew where the house with the red-tile roof was. It couldn't take ten minutes to drive there—even less if she speeded, which she most certainly intended to do.

Chapter 6

Okay, Lily thought as she charged up the steps to the library, *nothing was going to go smoothly today.* She'd found Barbara Marr's house, but not Webster Renbarcker. "Web" was at the library, his cousin claimed. She often dropped him off to spend a couple hours there. If Lily wanted to find Mr. Renbarcker, she needed to go there.

So she had.

She swung open the heavy library door, fretting that this was going to be a whole wasted morning, when she could have been with Griff. What she'd risked that morning—what she wanted to risk with him again—made her wonder if she was losing her mind.

Chasing an old man who might not even talk with her seemed another symptom of insanity—yet she only took a few steps into the old, cool library to feel bombarded by a flush of great memories. Her dad had often brought the girls here—likely to give their mom a break, Lily thought now—but as a child she'd only known those mornings as a special treat. The smell of books, the tall windows letting in the long, yellow ribbons of light, the quiet, the big chairs that a little girl could curl up in… she'd loved it all when she was a child.

Still did. The old blue rug looked the same, so did the giant, oak library desk. It was impossible not to feel safe here. She ambled through aisles in the adult section, not certain what Webster Renbarcker looked like—but for sure, he had to be a senior.

There was no one over fifty in adult fiction, or in the reference room in back. Disappointed, she just glanced in the childrens' room, even as she was aiming for the back door…and there he was. An older man with longish white hair and scratchy white whiskers was sitting on a cushioned stool, leafing through a child's picture book.

A couple kids huddled in the corner with an older sister; a mom and toddler had claimed the sunny spot under a window. Lily quietly approached the older man, said gently, "Mr. Renbarcker?"

He immediately looked up with faded blue eyes.

"My name is Lily Campbell. I used to live here. My dad used to work at your mill."

He brightened up as if she'd given him a present. Once he started talking, he couldn't seem to stop. He tended to fade out now and then, but the past seemed clearer to him than the present.

"Never thought I'd see any of you Campbells again. Your daddy never set that fire, honey. He loved the mill.

He loved me. He'd been watching out for me from before I got sick, watched out for my wife the same way."

It was as if the old man's heart hurt. Words just poured out of him.

"He knew I was sick, your daddy, because he found me on the floor one day. I'd had some kind of seizure. He was just a boy then, almost fresh out of college. Had a young wife—your mama, prettiest thing I've ever seen, she was. I didn't have a son. Didn't have any children. Couldn't. Maybe my body knew I was going to get sick, you think?"

"I don't know, sir."

"The thing was…your daddy, he covered for me, every which way from Sunday. I made mistakes. He tried to catch them. I'd be fine one day, selling the farm the next, sending shipments to Canada instead of Louisiana, I could get that goofy. I couldn't face it. Couldn't believe it. Hid it from my wife as long as I could. I thought I was crazy."

"It sounds so frightening, Mr. Renbarcker."

"It was. It was. That was just the thing. I didn't know it was an illness in the beginning, or for a long while. I just thought I was losing my mind. Your dad was better than a son to me. I loved him. I loved your mama, too."

Lily felt tears well. Good tears. Loved tears.

"When it got real bad…well, I'm sure you know. I lost the mill. It had to be closed. I'd mucked up far more than your father could fix. But when they said he was despondent over losing his job—honey, it wasn't like that at all. He knew I was sick. He knew what was coming.

There was no shock to him, no sudden surprise. He knew we were going down."

Lily suddenly couldn't breathe. For the first time, she was talking to someone who knew her dad back then. Who was describing her dad as a good man—a hero, not a coward. A man who'd never had a "depressed" reason to set that fire—or any other fire.

"We'd talked about it many times, Lily. I urged him to quit and leave me with my own problems. He had you three girls by then—and nothing he adored more than his daughters. He had to be worried about finances, yet when I told him to leave me, find another job, he said that you girls loved mac and cheese, and none of you needed a fancy car. He'd saved. Enough to knuckle down and find himself another job when that had to be, but he was sticking by me to the end. You know what bothered me most, young lady?"

"Tell me," Lily urged him.

But the old man suddenly leaned forward with a wheezing cough, and when he finally straightened again, there seemed a hazy fog over his eyes. "Danielle, did you make me some of your famous huckleberry pie for dinner tonight?" He winked. "You look so pretty today, my dear. I love that color of blue on you."

"I...thank you." She'd learned so much. She wanted to get to her cell phone, call her sisters. Wanted to figure out what all this information meant—if her dad had never set that long-ago fire, then who *had?* And did that have anything to do with the two fires since she'd come back to town?

And then there was Griff. She wanted to get back

with him, to see what was happening to his store, to dig into whatever she could help him with. And yeah, to dig into whatever crazy place they were going personally together, too.

But she couldn't just up and leave the older man. Mr. Renbarcker wasn't thinking straight. She didn't know if or when his cousin would come looking for him. The mom and her toddler had wandered off; the clutch of other kids had been picked up by their father. Another group of kids popped in. Mr. Renbarcker kept talking to "Danielle" as if Lily were the one and only love of his life.

A boisterous group of tweeners piled in the doors, girls, giggling loud enough to raise the dead, finally arousing the librarian to stand in the doorway with a frown. It was the first thing that had distracted Mr. Renbarcker, who finally looked at her and said, "I know you, don't I?"

Putting a solution in motion seemed to take forever. The librarian, Sarah-Leigh Jenkins, was enlisted to track down Barbara Marr's phone number, but Sarah seemed to think it was suspicious for Lily to take an interest in the old man. Lily managed to reach Barbara Marr; but really, it was easiest just to drive the older man back home, since he was willing to get in the car with her—even if the librarian was scandalized all over again. Driving him was just faster than waiting for his cousin to get there, and Lily couldn't fathom why anyone would think anything was hokey about a young woman being kind to someone elderly.

Only, by then, outside, it was hot enough to fry bacon on the pavement. Her rental car's air conditioner coughed and sputtered like a pneumonia case.

She got Mr. Renbarcker back to his relatives, then *finally* was free to drive back to Griff's. By then she was frustrated and itchy-hot, and verging on cranky. Her cell phone registered five calls—all from her sisters. Admitting to Cate why she'd come back to Pecan Valley this summer had clearly alerted her sisters' alarm bells. Now there'd be no end to their advice. And she'd call them both back.

But not yet. Right then, she just wanted Griff.

"Hey, Griff, I just want to…"

"Griff, what do you think of…"

"Griff, how can I…?"

Griff considered hurling out the back and beating his head on the closest rock. He'd been patient all morning, but at this point he was hot, cranky, frustrated and just plain fed up. There were too many problems—all of which needed addressing immediately. There were way too many questions with no answers, and a zillion people hovering every damn time he had a chance to dig in.

This time, when he turned around there was Mrs. Georgia Maryweather, four-foot-eleven in heels and a ribboned hat, holding a peach-pecan pie. "Griff, I felt certain you'd need a little pick-me-up, bless your heart. The mister and I, we were so sorry to hear about the fire. It sure is a mess."

"What a kind thing to do. Thank you, Mrs. Maryweather."

Griff gave himself credit. He didn't blow his temper, because of course he'd never bellow at a sweet old woman. Or a crotchety old woman. Or any woman. As anyone in town knew, he didn't have a temper. He was low-key, never moved fast, never expressed anger.

Damned if he would behave like his dad. Ever. No matter what the provocation.

Mrs. Maryweather, of course, wanted a complete, chatty version of what had happened, who did it, what the damage would cost, what she and Mr. Maryweather could do to help, when he'd have the store back in business, the problem with young people today, the terror of crime and the story of her sister's daughter's cousin's break-in last year.

Griff could feel the start of a tic in his right eye. His stomach had shrunk to the size of a small, tight knot. Early-afternoon heat had come in like a prize-fighter, fast and sharp, a hot blow that could fell anybody.

"Now, Griff, sugar, you just tell me if you…"

"Griff…?"

For four hours now, he hadn't accomplished anything substantial. Couldn't finish a conversation. Couldn't end a sentence. Either the cell phone was buzzing or a fresh batch of people showed up. It wasn't as if this was the fire of the century. It was just a mess.

"Now, Mr. Maryweather and I, we'd—"

A sudden movement caught his attention—the shine of glossy brown hair braiding through the crowd. Lily. Ignoring everyone, including a few accusing stares directed her way, she seemed solely focused on him, his face, his expression. Herman Conner, who'd been unshakable all morning, hitched up his trousers and aimed to block her path.

But nothing was stopping Lily. She barged past elbows and looks and conversation, the frown on her brow deepening as she finally reached him. "I'm really sorry. I assumed I could get here a lot earlier. I got caught up."

"Nothing to be sorry about," he assured her. "In fact, I should have called your cell, told you to forget it. There's nothing anyone can do to help me right now."

She searched his face, barely whispered, "Yeah, right." And then, in a sudden loud soprano, "Griff, I'm feeling sick with the heat. Could you just help me sit down for a minute? I'm afraid I'm going to faint."

She wasn't going to faint. He couldn't imagine why she'd pull such a drama, grabbing his arm, lifting her other hand to her forehead like a swooning Scarlett O'Hara. It was the hokiest acting job he'd ever seen… but he couldn't be 100% positive of that. Lily *did* have trouble with heat, and it wasn't as if he could ignore a woman asking for his help.

Much less Lily.

He'd have brought her into the nearest air-conditioning—which was the shop next door—but somehow Ms. Drama Queen, even as she moaned and groaned, elbowed him around the side of the store, down the alley, to a patch of shade. Faster than a snake, she wiggled through her purse and emerged with two water bottles. The first one she opened and poured over his head before he could even think about sputtering.

The second, she handed him for a drink. "Sit," she said.

"What the hell are you doing?" He pushed a hand through his dripping hair, refusing to enjoy the sudden burst of cool. Although Lily couldn't possibly know it, there were certain things Griff never did. Obey orders was one of them. Allow himself to be "handled" was another.

"We're going to cool you down and calm you down. Or you can vent a bunch of yelling on my head, if you'd rather. Both choices are okay with me."

"What?"

"Griff, you looked seriously ready to explode."

"I'm fine."

"Yeah? I'm a teacher. I told you that. I work with gifted students. I think I told you that, too. Extra-bright kids." She nudged the cold water bottle toward him again and couldn't help miss how he glared at her, but still, he took a long, long pull. "I'm used to knowing when they're going to blow."

"I don't blow."

"Of course you blow. Everybody gets angry sometimes."

"I couldn't be less angry."

"Right. See, my kids—they're used to high expectations put on them. They're used to meeting those expectations, getting a thrill when they even do more. But when they can't quite make that A-plus grade, they can go through a mighty crash. They hate it."

"I'm not one of your kids, Lily. And I sure as hell don't need caretaking. By anyone."

"There's no reason in the universe why you can't come unglued now and then."

There sure as hell was. His father capitalized every reason why a man—A Good Man—expected control from himself. Always. No exceptions. No discussion. "I'm not unglued."

She didn't take a breath, didn't look patient, didn't keep pushing the psychology crap. He had to get back to that infernal commotion, he knew that. He'd been talking all morning, couldn't waste time on any more useless talk. Stuff had to be *done.*

But somehow—not because he was unraveling or unglued or any nonsense like that—he did spill a little. "Everyone's talking about the fire. Hell, me, too. It's arson. That's damned upsetting, but reality is still… there are some practical things that have to be done. I got hooked up to a temporary generator, but it doesn't have enough juice for what I need in the back room. Debbie—of Debbie's Diner—has taken the fresh ice cream, going to sell at the restaurant. But I've got my batch freezers, my barrel freezers, the high-sheen blenders, the flavor tanks. All the equipment it takes to make and test serious ice cream. I don't care about some stupid financial loss. It's the mess. It's—"

She interrupted. "I get it. So what do you need first? An electrician to work on the power? Or do you need to move the equipment? Have to find a place? What?"

"It's sort of…all of the above. I need some straight information—from an electrician, a plumber—before I can make a move. But every time I turn around, there's a dozen people, the police, Herman, the insurance investigator...my kids. The darned kids are so worried they can't stay out of it, but I—"

"Okay." She lurched to her feet. "You stay here. Sit, drink some water, rehydrate, use your cell. I'll take care of the boys. Between the three of us, we'll run interference for you. You get done what you need to get done."

He frowned.

She cocked her head. "What?"

"You pulled this last night and it was reasonably cute, but enough's enough. You're manipulating me. Handling me."

She rolled her eyes. "As if I could. Relax, Griff. I'm not the manipulator type."

She charged off, leaving him in the cool shade with the water, staring after her. She was right, of course. He'd never met anyone less of a manipulator type than Lily.

But something fishy was definitely going on. He could feel it. His stomach had de-clenched. The tic had disappeared. He'd lost the freaked-out feeling.

That woman was downright *dangerous*.

But then he took another cool slug of water and hunkered down with his cell phone.

Dangerous.

Lily.

Pairing those two words created an oxymoron if ever there was one. He liked her. Possibly he way more than liked her. He was downright fascinated by how powerfully and unexpectedly he was attracted to her—got a real click when they were talking. Got more than a click when they were touching.

But she wasn't dangerous.

She was in danger.

And he damned well better keep that priority on the front line.

By four that afternoon, Lily was blister-hot, savagely hungry, and having a terrific time. The boys, Jason and Steve, had worked with her like parts of a well-honed team. Initially, she'd sent them off with money to buy ice, cups, water. She'd scared up a card table from the business next door and set the whole thing up to work as a barrier between Griff and the bystanders. Those still curious could congregate, but they couldn't get to him—at least not without interference, and the boys were pit-bull-protective that way.

She had a feeling no one had trusted Jason with personal cash in…forever, because he counted back every penny of change, braced as if expecting her to accuse him of lifting a cut. When she praised both boys for helping to protect Griff, they both grew five inches—at least—and walked around with the posture of soldiers.

It was enough to give a teacher heart palpitations. Man, it felt good to see a beaten-down kid try on some self-esteem.

Okay, so maybe the afternoon wasn't all peaches and cream. The sheriff insisted on taking both boys aside, grilling them on where they'd been at every hour of the night before, and whether they could prove it. Herman Conner had pointed a finger at her and said, "Honey, you and I are going to have a little talk later," which put a mosquito in her stomach.

That wasn't the only icky part of the afternoon. Griff's fire had lowered her popularity points, and it wasn't as if she had been batting a thousand before last night. Still, being out and about was a way to talk with people. Listen. Ask questions. She discovered others who'd known her mom and dad—and others who'd worked at the mill before it closed.

A hefty truck pulled in the back alley and started loading out what was, she assumed, Griff's fancy equipment. A few guys hung with him for a while, scuffling the dirt, hands on hips, jawing plans and problems. By the time the truck rumbled off and Griff aimed for her, she was being confronted by three redheads.

She'd already met Mary Belle—the buxom redhead who ran Belle Hair—at the grocery store. But this afternoon she had her two daughters with her, not that that relationship needed explaining. The teenagers looked just like their mama—lots and lots of eye makeup. Major breasts, displayed in sweetheart tees. Heaven knew what hair color they'd all been born with, but new-age red was obviously adopted as their family color of choice.

"Lily, sugar, I wish you'd let me do something about that hair," Mary Belle told Lily.

"I'm dying to get it cut. I just honestly haven't had time," Lily said, which was 95 percent true. The only holdback was a sincere worry what Mary Belle might do with a pair of scissors.

"I could give you some real style, honey. Jazz you

up some. You need a little more…" Mary Belle made a motion with her hands "…style, if you want to appeal to a man like Griff."

"Pardon?"

"It's all right, Lily. I hear everything in the salon. No point in trying to keep gossip from me. And bless his heart, I tried to catch him myself—when I was between husbands, anyhow. Never did work, even though I know he wanted to try." Mary Belle cocked her head. "Anyhow—y'all give me a call in the morning, I'll get you in, and that's a promise. I'll do you myself. Trained in Savannah, you know…well, hello, handsome."

Griff came up behind them, greeted Mary Belle's coy flash of eyelashes and inviting smile with his usual Southern boy charm. But Lily had long figured out he could flirt in his sleep; it didn't mean anything beyond an unshakeable kindness to women. Behind the courtesy, though, she could see the tired circles under his eyes, the smudges of dirt that tracked his clothes, dusted his shoes. He was one wiped-out cookie.

Still, he looked better than earlier, when she'd worried he was absolutely at the end of his rope—even though he'd denied it to the death. She wouldn't make *that* mistake again, suggesting he had human qualities, like anger and frustration. Those sharp edges were definitely gone. Now he just looked as if he could crash the instant he sat down—if given the chance.

Lily had been thinking about that all day. Whether she was going to give him that chance to rest.

Or whether she was going to do something she'd never

done in her life. Take a petrifying risk. Hurl good sense
to the winds. And make love with a man for no reason
beyond that she terribly, totally, irrevocably…

Wanted to.

Chapter 7

"So you finally get to escape from here?" she asked him.

"*Finally* is the operative word." Griff couldn't believe she'd stuck it out through the whole afternoon.

"Hey! Quit looking at me! I'm wilted. More than wilted. Hair went flat, clothes went wrinkled, the whole body went droopy."

"You're kidding, right?" She looked beautiful. The more he was around her, the more he was becoming addicted to the fresh cheeks and huge, dark eyes, and all that thick, silky hair. She wasn't just beautiful. She was damned close to impossibly appealing. "Wait a minute. You weren't listening to Mary Belle, were you? Promise me now, you'll never let that woman get near you with a pair of scissors."

She chuckled. "I'm desperate for a major trim, but

I'm an easy cut. Otherwise, that woman's sense of style would be more than a little…daunting."

He laughed—for the first time all day. And realized that his neck and shoulders were unknotting for the first time all day, too. He steered her under the overhang, for the shade, aiming for his EOS. "Thanks for hanging out this afternoon. Couldn't have been fun. I owe you."

"Yup, you do. I expect diamonds and rubies and stuff. But for right now, I have a more immediate plan."

"What?"

"You drop me off at the B and B. I'm going to shower and crash. You go straight home, turn off all phones, and crash yourself."

He waited. "That's the whole plan?"

"Well, maybe you should also lock your door so nobody can bug you."

"Hmm. I have a different plan."

"What?"

They reached his car. He clipped open her door. "I drive you to your B and B. You get a change of clothes— like a swimsuit, a towel. We go back to my place. We can either shower first, or skip the shower and head straight for the hot tub—but I have in mind putting ice cubes in it. Have something ice-cold to drink. Followed by something ice-cold to eat."

"All right, all right, all right. You can have me. Body and soul, and skip the rubies. Just the words *ice cold* are enough to bring sentimental tears to my eyes."

"You're easy, Lily."

"Yeah. I've been told that before."

He'd bet the bank she hadn't. He'd bet the bank

there'd never been one thing any guy had ever found easy about Lily…which might be part of the reason he was so damned mesmerized.

At the B and B, she only took a few minutes, flew out the door with Louella flapping on her tail, urging a plate of cookies on her, talking nonstop, waving wildly at him.

He only had eyes for Lily. She dropped a sack in the backseat—big enough to hold a bathing suit and changes of clothes. But somehow, in those few minutes upstairs, she'd turned into another woman. The shorts had been replaced by a sundress, all white and yellow, the daisies at the hem fluttering around her knees.

Her legs were bare.

Her eyes were softer than chocolate.

Her lips were noticeably free of lipstick.

And she'd pulled up all that thick, silky hair with combs.

"What?" she said, when she piled in and yanked on her seat belt. Instead of starting the car, she'd caught him looking at her.

"Nothing. Just wiped out after that long day," he said, but tiredness was the last thing on his mind. He kept trying to remind himself that she was a teacher. Not that teachers couldn't be gorgeous, but it was hard to think of them as femme fatales. And that was just it. She wasn't. He could readily picture her in front of a bunch of kids, laughing, scolding, hugging the little ones, playing games. Not seducing guys. Not making guys melt at her feet just for a smile.

Yet somehow, there was something in her eyes, the way she looked at him, the way she smiled at him—that messed with his head.

Was *still* messing with his head.

He had to make another stop to pull off the rest of his evening plan, but within an hour they were back at his place. The hot tub was set on lukewarm, the pool jutting over the hilltop. She emerged from her shower with a towel concealing her suit, and immediately saw the spread on the patio table. Plates and bowls were set in a bed of ice. Fresh shrimp with a sharp red dip. Chilled chardonnay. A plate of cheese, crackers and caviar. Lime sorbet in a sterling icer. Fresh peaches. It wasn't exactly a normal dinner, but the food was all bite-size, no fuss.

"That's it," she said. "I'm in love with you. I know, I know, that's what all the ladies say."

"It is. I can't help if I'm wonderful."

"Yeah, that's your press all right." She plopped the towel on a lounge chair, touched a bare foot to test the temperature in the tub, and then sank in with a groan loud enough to wake the sky. "Speaking of your press, though—I heard under the table that you're some kind of high-brow math whiz."

There, for a moment, he felt reassured. She wasn't perfect. In fact, when she started prying and probing and using that weird intuition of hers, she could be downright annoying. He didn't have to worry about a permanent attachment to a woman who just never let anything rest. Right? "Hey, I already confessed I had a degree in math."

"Yeah, but you never said you used it to do really top-secret, fancy work."

"Who told you such an outrageous story?" Apparently, he wasn't supposed to notice how fast she'd dipped that curvy figure out of sight. He could pretend when he had to.

"I never kiss and tell. But I picked it up from a lot of sources. There was a tall, gray-haired woman—your insurance agent? I heard her talking about making sure all your math computers were extra-protected at home, that maybe you needed more coverage or security for your work in progress. Then one of the kids—I think Jason—was telling the other boy who works for you about how you were going to cure 'really, really bad diseases' with math. How you were working for somebody in secret—"

"Sheesh," he said disgustedly. He popped a cold shrimp in her mouth, handed her a sweating-cold chardonnay, and slipped into the water himself. The lukewarm water hit his battered, knotted muscles like a balm. Still, he turned a scowl her way.

"It's all right, Griff. Don't worry. I'm just a lowly teacher. I didn't understand anything, really."

"You managed to add two and two and come up with different answers than almost anyone knows around here."

"Why is it a secret?"

Another reassurance, he thought. She wasn't just smart. And nosy. She could be downright relentless—so relentless that he couldn't think of a single way to avoid answering her. "If someone was working on, say, a hopeful new medicine—a drug that could cure a serious type of disease—then that medicine could conceivably be worth a lot of money. So it might make the most sense, security-wise, for the computations and analyses, and all the trick problems associated with mathematically testing the possibilities, to be done off-site. It's mostly computer work. Calculations, probabilities, that kind of thing. There's no reason it has to be done in an office or inside company walls. In fact, it's probably better done in a private facility, where there are no distractions in sight, no one tempted to steal it." He looked at her. "Particularly if no one has a clue where such work is being done."

She took a bite of the cracker mounded with caviar, grimaced, gulped down some wine, and aimed for the tray of cheeses. "It's just hard to grasp," she admitted. "That your ice-cream parlor is such a front."

"It's not a front." She'd offended him again. Not just because his ice-cream deal was real, but because a "front" implied gangster-type behavior. Like he had something to hide that was wrong.

"Okay, okay, bad choice of words," she said gently. "It's still difficult to grasp. You're so adorable, it's just really hard to think of you as being geeky. *Major* geeky."

Okay. He'd had enough of her playing with him. He'd stuffed down enough food, had quenched his thirst, was de-stressed from the frustrating day. He had more than enough energy to tackle her now. "You said you'd had quite a morning, that something happened…"

"It did." There, that wicked grin of hers faded out. She leaned her head back, sank in water to her neck. "I talked to Mr. Renbarcker—the man who owned the mill back when?"

He listened—to how she'd managed to discover Webster Renbarcker was in town, how she'd located him, what he'd had to say. He watched her face, watching her expression lift on hearing what a good man her father was, what good care he'd taken of the sick mill owner.

"And that's just the thing, Griff. Mr. Renbarcker was positive my father would never have set a fire. My dad loved the mill, loved him, loved us. Mr. Renbarcker talked about how my dad was prepared to stay to the end, that he'd socked away a financial safety net.... So it doesn't make sense that my dad felt such despair when the mill closed. He *knew* it was going to close. He *knew* how sick Mr. Renbarcker was. There was nothing to throw him into a depression. If anything, he no longer had to feel responsible, but was finally free to go on and do something else."

By sheer strength of will, Griff refrained from adjusting the shoulder strap of her suit that had accidentally sneaked off her shoulder. On the serious subject at hand though, he felt he had to caution her. "Your dad still could have accidentally set that fire, sugar."

"Well, the first thing that mattered to me was clearing his name, getting that cloud off his reputation, that he'd be a man who'd set a fire for money. But the second issue, about whether he could have accidentally set it—that's just a plain *no*. My dad was a total perfectionist around his wood shop. We girls were never allowed near the varnishes or chemicals. He didn't have a careless bone in his whole body. There could be no accidental fire, not with my dad." She sighed, leaned her head back. "But I realize that I can't prove that."

"But that's all right, isn't it? You didn't come thinking you'd find information that would lead you to a court of law. I think you came to prove in your own mind what happened. That the fire wasn't your father's fault. And it sounds as if you're doing exactly that."

"I am. And it couldn't feel better. I always believed my dad was a hero. That's what he *was,* Griff. A terrific man. You'd have liked him, honestly."

"I don't doubt it."

What a night it had turned into. The sucking heat of the day had finally eased. The sky was deepening, darkening. Even the birds had gone silent, and stars buttoned the sky with fancy silver studs. It was a night to romance her, not dwell on troubling subjects…but he liked it that she trusted him enough to talk about this. "Lily, I'm really surprised that you three sisters were separated."

"There wasn't a choice. No one could take all three of us."

"I understand how suddenly adding three children could be a financial burden for a foster family. But I've lived here for several years now, long enough to know folks. Even if you had to be separated, fostered in different homes, I'd think an effort would have been made for you to stay in Pecan Valley. Your home. Instead of being shifted all over the country. I'd think normally, that a social service agency or court would think it best to keep you around people who knew you, where you didn't have to be uprooted from schools and friends and all."

She considered. "I don't know. As a little girl, I didn't think of it as a question. It's just the way it was. But Sophie and Cate and I all felt the same. Because of that fire, we not only lost our mom and dad, but each other. It was…traumatically lonely. I'm not kidding."

"I don't doubt it—and that's just the point. This is a community that comes together. Yeah, there are weird folks, just like anywhere else. Plenty of problems. But it's hard for me to believe that the authorities didn't try and keep you three together."

"Maybe they did, and I just didn't know. Anyway, that's water over the dam. And there's something else I want to bring up with you."

"Okay. Shoot."

"It's a little…awkward."

"That's okay." He didn't know what she was going to say, but he was increasingly troubled. Nothing was adding up. There seemed no explanation—or source—for the buzz of gossip blaming Lily for the current fires, for her being "like her dad." There seemed more and more unanswered questions about the fire from her childhood—and no explanations at all for why there'd been two arson fires since she came back to town.

The more that happened, the more Griff felt he was missing something. That Lily was missing something. And that, if this situation escalated any further, someone could be hurt—or killed, just like in that long-ago fire.

They had to figure out what was going on.

He leaned forward, thinking to turn off the jets of

water. They'd both been in the tub long enough to be waterlogged. He was thinking about fires and problems, thinking about what awkward thing she was going to spring on him—when suddenly, in a swoop of water and slick, warm arms, she slid against him. Bared her neck to press her wet, soft lips against his.

An explosion couldn't have startled him more.

Slinky as a mermaid, she folded herself against him, water lapping the tops of her breasts when she slip-slid onto his lap. Her left hand slowly stroked up his arm, feeling the slope of his shoulders, then sliding around his neck. Her next kiss was a naked offer. An invitation.

His brain was sucked under so fast he couldn't remember how to breathe. "Hey," he managed. "What started this?"

"You were frowning," she said. "And I decided you'd had enough to frown about today."

"I can't argue with that."

"I'm sick of trouble and worrying. I've been knee deep since I got here. I'm tired of it." Her voice didn't sound remotely tired. She nibbled down his neck as she continued to...*discuss.*

"Me, too."

"So I think it would be a good idea to do something that erases all that trouble and stress from our minds."

He did, too. He'd even had seducing her in mind, if not tonight, then imminently soon. He just didn't expect... well. His wholesome, fresh-faced teacher was skidding strokes down his chest, through wet hair, over appendix scar, past navel, down, right into his trunks. Her slim hand found him, painted agony down the length of him with her fingertip, then closed around him. Tight. Snug. Owning him.

"Why," he murmured, "am I worried right now?"

"Because I'm a very scary woman? A woman who's about to take away all your choices. All your stress. All your responsibility. It's going to be hard for you to deal with it."

"It's already hard."

"Yeah. I noticed." The smile she shot him wasn't Lily's. The arch of her brow, the sneaky smile, then the way she slipped the bathing suit straps off her shoulders—this wasn't a woman he could trust. This wasn't anyone he'd let into his life before. This was a woman who could start fires in a man that, just maybe, no one in heaven or hell could put out.

"Lily—"

"Uh-uh. No talking. I like talking to you. I even love talking to you. But right now, this isn't about you, Griff. It's about me. This is the summer when I get to stand up and take what's mine." She lifted her head just after taking a small nip out of shoulder. "You don't have to be mine next year or next week or tomorrow. Just right now."

Okay, okay. He knew she was talking big. It wasn't her normal nature to do one-nighters, to throw all caution to the wind, to not give a damn about consequences. And although he wasn't exactly infamous for mentioning consequences to a woman he wanted, he invariably took care of things so there weren't any. Right now, though, they were in the hot tub, and if anything was supposed to happen or going to happen, he assumed it'd happen in the bedroom, where he had protection.

Where he had control, for that matter.

Right then, he could have used some control.

Somewhere a phone rang. Somehow she coaxed him out of the water, onto the flat deck surface, where their wet, slick bodies cleaved from chest to thigh, belly to belly, lips to lips. At some time, the sky had lost all color, gone silky black and dangerously concealing. And his blood seemed to be pumping from a hot, dark well.

He couldn't catch his breath. It was the woman who was supposed to feel that way, not the guy. Sure as hell, not a guy like him, who'd enjoyed women from the day he was born—so the problem was her. The difference was her.

The danger was her.

She kissed. Rubbed. Danced against him with her breasts, her pelvis, the hum in the back of her throat. She reached something…lonely inside of him. Something needy and sharp. Something beyond sex and pleasure.

The deck was hard; he shifted so his weight wasn't driving her into that bruising surface. It was just a matter of twisting them around, but he heard her guttural laugh when she climbed on top. It was a chuckle of power. Maniacal female power.

Yet he saw the innocence in her face. The flush of shock and pleasure when he tightened his hips, stroked upward with infinite care until she was seated tight on him. Then came the ride, unlike any other. Her eyes turned soft and lost, focusing on him, only on him.

You'd think she'd never done this.

You'd think he hadn't. He sure as hell couldn't remember anything like this, ever, not the need—clawing with feral desperation. Not the emotional connect—like he'd die if he couldn't have her, couldn't be with her, like this, forever. Not the scalping blade of pleasure—ripping through him, tearing fast, shredding any knowledge he'd had of release in the past.

He called her name.

She called his right back.

Yearning swept over him like a tidal wave—her scent, her sounds, her taste, her textures, sending him into an uncontrollable tumble of sensation. She rode that wave with him, rocketing them both on the same shore of wildly intense release.

When it was finally over he closed his eyes, aware he was breathing like a freight train, loud and heavy. Maybe he could move for a tornado, but he doubted it.

His hands moved before the rest of him. His hands instinctively started making long, slow, soothing strokes on the body on top of him. Lily was draped all over him.

"Are either of us alive?" he murmured.

"Oh, I am. And I don't know why I ever bothered having sex before you. Why didn't you tell me it could be this good?"

"Because I didn't know you? Because I didn't know it could be this good either?"

"Yeah, right. I'll bet you tell that to all the girls."

"I've never told anyone that. Ever." Which was true. And should have been enough to scare the socks off him.

Whatever was happening with Lily scaled mountains he'd never before climbed.

"Hey, weren't you paying attention? I just seduced you. And personally, I think I did a fabulous job of it."

"You sound mighty smug."

"I feel mighty smug."

"You should. You were the sexiest, most extraordinary lover I've ever imagined or dreamed of."

She gave him a smile, but she pushed off his chest faster than lightning. "Okay. This being sweet to each other has gone on long enough."

He didn't think so. She was up in a sudden flash, with a smack and a laugh and a race for the shower, making major noises about what an exhausting day he'd had, so she was headed back to the B and B so he could get some real rest. Griff felt as if he'd been doused with cold water.

Lily was totally fine. Funny. Warm. It was just… mountains had just moved, so how come she hadn't noticed? Why wasn't she guiding conversation toward "what it all meant", and what should happen next, what she wanted, what he wanted, all that female talk that always—*always*—followed making love.

The truth was, he *wanted* that chatter. He never had before, but he did now.

As fast as she climbed out of the shower, he started trailing after her, trying to talk her out of going back to the B and B. "Why can't you just stay here?"

"Because, first off, I don't have any fresh clothes. More important, you're starting your day tomorrow with a lot to do related to your fire and your ice-cream business and all. And third, you had a seriously awful day today, and you really need sleep. You think you'll sleep if I'm here?"

"I don't want to sleep." He heard the plaintive boy tone in his voice, but hell. Why did he have to be mature all the time? "We could just sleep," he promised.

She just looked at him—en route to the car. By then, the dishes were done, the towels all hung up, the cover back on the hot tub. It was irritating that she took better care of his stuff than he did. And he was still shadowing her heels like a lovesick puppy.

In the car, she finally got around to mentioning what was wrong. "Griff," she said softly, "I feel responsible."

"For what?"

"For the fire at your ice-cream place."

"Huh? Did you forget something? You were with me. There's no way in hell you could be responsible, sugar."

"Maybe not technically. But this was the second fire since I came home. Of course I didn't set them. But they both have a personal link to me. The first, because it was the mill. And the second could be—I'm mighty scared—because you've taken me on publically as a friend. Which makes me feel guiltier than a Judas. I don't know why there's a link to me, but there seems to be. And sheesh, I'm miserably, miserably sorry—"

Because it only took two stupid shakes to get to her B and B, he was stuck pulling in the drive. Louella had left the porch light on, undoubtedly for Lily. Moths were dancing in the light. Heat seeped in the shadows. Cicadas were singing from every bush. He walked her to the bottom of the wide old veranda, and when she wouldn't let up on how guilty she felt, he just swung her in his arms. He kissed her.

Then kissed her again.

Then kissed her again.

Then just wrapped his arms around her and held on. He felt her silky hair against his cheek and neck, inhaled the warmth and smallness and sweetness of her. There was the oddest intimacy in just...holding. He could feel the shape of her breasts beneath the sundress, had an absolute, clear recollection of the breasts he'd laved with his tongue, their plumpness, the taste, how she'd arched her back with a cry at a certain, tiny bite. All those fresh memories came on lush in his head. Everything about her naked body, how he'd felt inside her. How she'd—

"Griff? Are you falling asleep up there?" She lifted her head, smiled at him from the shadows.

"I just don't want to leave you." There'd never been a simpler truth.

"I'll see you tomorrow. Or the first moment you have time. But right now, go home, get some serious rest. That's an order."

"Lily." He said her name, heard the promise and wonder in his voice. He wanted to tell her he'd fallen in love, but he could see from her expression, her eyes, that she wouldn't believe him. Not now. Not yet. So he just left it like that, with her name spoken into the night air. He pressed his lips to her brow, and then climbed into his EOS and drove back home.

* * *

On the quiet road, the windows open to feel fresh wind on his face, he thought about what she'd said. Lily had no factual basis to believe the two recent fires were linked to her—but he believed the same. Something was wrong. Badly wrong.

People were whispering about Lily, had been from the moment she arrived, and the gossip had taken an extra-dark turn that day. It stopped when he'd turned his head or turned around, but he'd heard tail ends of it through the daylight hours—that "someone" had said how Lily was "like her dad". That fire setting was "in the blood".

It was completely ridiculous.

Besides which, it was completely wrong.

But someone—or a bunch of someones—was putting that talk out there. It was being said, being spread.

He wanted to ignore it, but it was starting to scare him.

Lily tiptoed into the B and B, slipped off her sandals, and trying not to breathe, or make any other sound, she hustled up the carpeted steps. Before she reached the top, she heard Louella call from below. "That you, Lily?"

"Yes, it's me."

"So you're home safe."

"You bet."

"Then I'm going to turn off the lights and lock up good. I don't like what's happening around this town, I don't. Can't understand a…" Her voice trailed down the shadowed hall, making Lily wonder if Louella actually talked 24-7, whether someone was there or not.

But her smile faded as she unlocked her room and slipped inside. The first time she'd seen the room, she'd loved it on sight. The mahogany four-poster, with its mound of soft, white pillows, was the-real-thing comfortable. Lace draped the long, skinny windows. Apparently like other houses this old, the bedroom had a sink against one wall, marble, gorgeous even if the mirror above it was cracked. She loved the room every time she walked in.

But right now, it was the last place in the universe she wanted to be.

She turned on the wheezy fan, shucked her clothes, switched off the light and crashed on the old percale sheets. She wanted to be with Griff, not here. The need to be with him bubbled up like a cry in her heart, a yearning coming from somewhere deep inside. Nothing like their lovemaking had ever happened to her before. It wasn't the sex.

Okay. It *was* a little bit about the stupendous sex.

But it was the other part that was even more stupendous—and dangerous. She'd felt so...*connected* to him. She hadn't let herself feel connected to anyone or anything, not deeply, since her family was torn apart after the fire. The losses had been too unbearable. Yet something about Griff reached her. He was alone the same way she was. She kept having the sense of her hand reaching his across a universe, finding the only other soul who might just understand her kind of loneliness.

She closed her eyes. Tried to sleep. When that failed,

she tried pacing the room in the dark. Then she tried brushing her hair, standing in front of the fan. When she still wasn't ready to sleep, she switched on the bedside lamp and turned on her laptop. She wasn't about to call her youngest sister in the middle of the night; she just sent her a short email, asking for a connect when Sophie had a chance.

Somewhere around four in the morning, Lily's body finally caved. She closed up, turned off, and tuned out. She'd just shut her eyes when her cell phone vibrated.

Sophie's voice was wide awake. "I've been worried to bits about you."

"What on *earth* are you doing up?"

"I know it sounds crazy, but it seems to be a newlywed thing. We start talking and can't stop. Mess around, fall asleep, start talking again. This love thing is exhausting. Now. Forget me. Fill me in."

Lily peeled out the whole story of her meeting with Mr. Renbarcker. The fires. How she'd come home to find out once and for all what caused their family fire, and hopefully to clear their dad's name. And she was finding answers, but those answers just seemed to lead to more troubling questions.

"The only truly wonderful thing so far, was talking with Mr. Renbarcker. Everything he said reminded me of dad. How dad was so happy. I remember him laughing, playing with us, being with us. The way his arm would loop around mom when we were all watching TV or walking in the park."

Sophie picked up that thought. "I could never believe

it, either. That dad could have caused that fire. But I didn't know if all of us were in denial."

"That's just it. Why I had to come back. I need to know the whole truth, whatever it is."

"Which is fine," her baby sister said. "Only, if you're finding out things that are making you afraid, I want you to get out of Dodge."

"No. That's not the real problem."

Sophie put on her bossy sister voice. "I hear fear in your voice, Lily."

"Because I'm petrified."

"That's it! Get out of there. Or I'll fly there—and get Cate to come with me. We'll both—"

Lily cut to the chase. "I'm not afraid about the fire. Or anything to do with the past. The problem is…well, it's a man."

"Say what?"

"A man."

Sophie tapped her phone, making Lily's ears pop. "Is this my sister talking? The schoolteacher who goes to jewelry parties and craft shows? The one who's idea of a fun evening is rereading Jane Austen?"

"He's all wrong for me. I'm going to leave. He's going to stay. He's got a long reputation for loving women and not committing. I never even passed an elementary course in flirting."

"You slept with him." Sophie didn't make it a question.

"It can't work. I totally know that. So I'm trying to just be cool, enjoy falling off the mountain before the crash.

Why can't I have a wild affair? You and Cate have been telling me to do it for years."

"Since when did you listen to us? You can't have a wild affair, because a wild affair isn't you."

"But maybe it is. Maybe for once in my life, I need to do exactly this. Have a completely irresponsible, hedonistic, dangerous, crazy sexy affair. Knowing there's no future. Just doing it because…because I've never wanted anything more. Never wanted anyone more."

"Then why are you scared?"

"What if I can't get over him? What if this is so… huge. This heart thing. This man. That no other guy will ever come close?"

"Okay. I'm trying to think reasonably here. I won't call Cate this second. I won't go out and buy a gun to shoot him. But that's what I want to do. If he hurts you, if he hurts you in even an eensy, tiny way—"

"Soph, everyone gets hurt. Nobody can save anybody that."

They were still talking, her sister's voice as familiar as her own heartbeat, their ways of talking and teasing, their codes as comforting as a band-aid on a sore. Neither were finished talking, when Lily abruptly ended the call.

Outside, she heard the sound of a fire engine siren.

Chapter 8

Lily raced over to the window. The siren sounded close—within blocks—but there was no sign of smoke or fire. Still, even through the trees and darkness she could see second-story lights popping on. Others had been awakened by the sound of the fire truck.

Her heart was thudding with dread, but she told herself not to panic.

She told herself that there was no reason to worry this had anything to do with her. That was pretty darned self-centered thinking. Everything wasn't about *her*.

Yet she whipped around, started searching for clothes. She'd just yanked a long-sleeved tee over her head when she sensed a sharp white flash of light, followed by a growl that made the whole house shake. Thunder. Lightning close enough to smell the ozone. Seconds later, rain slashed in the west windows, making the curtains dance and shake.

She pushed down the windows, turned and promptly hit her knee on the four-poster in the dark. She found underpants, shorts—though she couldn't see what color—bent down, groped for her sandals. She could still hear the sirens. Her heart pounded as uncontrollably as a child's nightmare. She rushed downstairs, almost tripping on the bottom step, and found Louella standing with her cane at the back screen door, wearing a housecoat and pink Crocs.

She'd lit a utility candle, put it in the sink, which illuminated just enough for Lily to find her way across the room.

"I'm glad you're here," Louella said. "You're my only tenant right now. I never mind that. But the house always feels bigger and creakier in a storm. I was worried how close that lightning was. Thought it might have hit the catalpa tree three doors down."

"Are you worried? Do you have a storm shelter?"

"Heavens no, honey. This is just a storm. It'll pass. Once that lightning's moved off to the east, I'll relax good and well." But there was worry in her eyes when she looked at Lily. "You heard the sirens?"

"Yes."

"I don't know what's going on in our town with these fires, but I have to say, it's starting to make me uneasy. I was told twice yesterday that I was making a mistake, letting a fire setter rent a room here. Of course, anyone listens to June Ellis should get their head examined. Damn fool woman married the biggest drinker in town, then whines about the mess she's in. So that's the kind of judgment *she's* got."

Lily's heart sank. Louella was staring out at the rain again, not at her. "Louella, do you want me to move?" she asked quietly.

"Lands sake, no. Lordamighty. You didn't think I'd believe silly talk like that, did you? Give me credit for some brains, honey. I took one look at your face and knew you had a good heart through and through."

"Thanks."

"Don't thank me for being smart. I was born smart. Can't take credit for it."

Lily had to smile, but it faded fast. "I don't want to cause you any trouble—"

"You couldn't cause me trouble if you tried. I'm a Southern magnolia, sugar. Southern women know how to be strong." Louella's gnarled hand circled Lily's wrist. "But I *am* worried about you."

"It's all right," Lily reassured her. "There's no reason to…"

Her voice trailed off when she saw the sheriff's car pull up to the curb.

Even in the gloomy storm, the flashing lights of the car were unmistakable.

Louella had the door open before Herman Conner was halfway up the veranda steps. "Why, Sheriff Conner," she started to say, but apparently the sheriff wasn't in a Southern, courteous mood.

He looked past Louella, saw Lily, motioned a come-on with his forefinger.

"You and I need to have a talk," he said curtly.

"Sure," she said. "How can I help?"

"You can *help* by getting in the car. I won't put cuffs on you if you just don't make a fuss. We'll talk at the station."

Lily's stomach clenched into a tight fist. "*What?* Are you telling me I'm under arrest?" She wanted to laugh. She really wanted to believe this was funny.

"Lily. Get your fanny in the car. I mean it. Now."

"Now, sheriff, there's no call to speak to Lily that way—"

"Louella, you stay out of this. I'm hot and I'm tired and I've had enough right now."

The station was as dark as everywhere else. Electricity was still down. Daylight was coming on, but the only thing easy to see was the stale coffee in yesterday's pot. Conner still poured himself a cold cup and offered her one. He motioned her into a back office with windows— not a jail—but the only place that had enough light to talk. The chairs were hard-core metal, the table a battered gray institutional type.

"Am I under arrest?" she finally had a chance to ask again.

Even in the poor light, she could see the hound-dog bags under Conner's eyes and the pallor of exhaustion behind his ruddy skin. The patience and kindness he'd shown her before was missing in a raw way. He was having trouble even meeting her eyes, was antsier than even she was.

"Darned if I know," he said. "I'm thinking on it. Don't tell me you didn't hear the sirens an hour ago."

"I did."

"The fire was in the library. Where you were yesterday."

"Oh, no—"

"Yeah. 'Oh no.' I'm getting tired of these oh-nos. You come in town, suddenly there's arson. Specifically, everywhere you've been. Sarah-Leigh, she's the head librarian—"

"I know." At his glare, Lily decided not to interrupt again.

"Sarah-Leigh saw you talking to Mr. Renbarcker at some length yesterday morning. She saw you in the childrens' section and in the adult section. She didn't specifically see you in the back reference room, but she didn't know of a soul who was back there yesterday, either. That's where the fire started. The old microfiche machines. The old newspaper records and archives."

"Oh, no," she said again.

"Just in case you didn't realize, this town thinks of the library as a treasure. And in case you didn't know, Griff's Secret is one of the favorite haunts in town. Everybody loves that ice cream. Then there was the first fire in the old mill, just days after you got here. At least there was no harm done in that one, but that's now three cases of arson. Three where a gasoline accelerant was used. And that's a for sure, because there were the same burn patterns in the debris, which is how we all know there was an ignitable liquid in a fire, but not diesel, because diesel burns a whole lot different than gasoline. I suspect you know all that. Because every one of those places has a connection to you. And the fire your daddy and mama were killed in, back when, was a gasoline-started fire, too. Now. What do you *expect* me to make of all this, Lily Campbell?"

"That this is awful. That this can't be coincidence."

"Well, now, we're sure on the same page there. So far, nobody's been hurt. It's just financial losses. Time, trouble, money. I put on an extra man these last few days, thankfully got to the library within two minutes of the alarm going off. Some records destroyed for sure, but nothing worse than that."

"Thank heavens," Lily breathed.

"No. There's no more 'thank heavens' in this story. I don't have, at this time, any concrete evidence to arrest you. But you're the one and only suspect. The only one with a connection to these arsons. The only one. You have anything you'd like to say about that?"

"I didn't do it, Sheriff. I've never set a fire in my life, anywhere, anytime. I teach school. You can check anything about my past you want, my school records, my work record. I had one speeding ticket when I was nineteen—that's all. You've talked to me. You've surely gotten a feel for my character—"

"Yes, I have, honey. I don't get any of this. None of us do. And I don't want to believe you're our arsonist, but I can't separate you from these crimes either. I'm not arresting you. Not this minute. But this would usually be the moment when I say you can't leave town—only, I'm real, real tempted to say the opposite. Get out of here. Go back to wherever you're from. Stay away from Pecan Valley. Don't show your head here again."

The lights suddenly popped on. An air conditioner

wheezed to life, and phones immediately started ringing. Lily hadn't answered the sheriff, didn't know what to say, when she suddenly saw Griff pushing through the heavy metal doors. He looked out of breath, wrinkled, unshaven and downright ticked off.

Griff gave her credit—more than credit. She held it together until he got her out in the fresh air, and then she leaned into him as if her spine suddenly turned liquid.

Getting his hands on her felt better than anything he could remember—better than air or water. Even better than sex. She clutched him tight enough to bruise. He let her. The rain had stopped, leaving a fresh-washed morning and Georgia sunshine so bright it stung the eyes.

Lily finally took a long breath and looked up at him. "I have to admit, being taken to a police station isn't the most fun way I've ever started a morning."

She clearly wanted him to smile. Unfortunately, he had to let her go when they reached his EOS, but he hustled her inside before anyone could conceivably get near her. Once he climbed in, he reached over to kiss her, just one hard, fast kiss, and then started the engine. His heart was pumping in thick, noisy thuds. His right hand made a white-knuckle fist on the steering wheel.

He wasn't angry, of course. He was just…a little tense. For a long time—maybe forever—he was going to have the picture in his head from when he'd walked into the police station and saw her. She was just sitting there, her face whiter than paper, Conner looming over her. Her dark eyes had looked rattled and lost and…

No, he wasn't mad.

But he was definitely tense.

Lily leaned back against the seat and closed her eyes, curled up as much as she could curl with the seat belt trapping her. Her palm pressed tight against her abdomen. "I can't swear, but I'm pretty sure I'm not cut out for a life of crime. There's still a chance, of course. But I don't think effective criminals would likely get this sick to their stomachs in a police station."

"You're not hurling in this car, sugar."

She chuckled. A watery chuckle, but still a chuckle. "You can always throw me out. I won't mind. All I want to do is curl up in a ball on the wet grass and talk myself into a nice, calm coma for a while."

He said casually, "How come Louella had to call me? Why didn't you call yourself?"

She opened one eye, studied his face. "It wasn't even five in the morning, Griff."

"So?" His voice was so smooth and calm, you could have spread it on toast. He was sure.

"So the sheriff just suddenly showed up in the middle of the storm. I had no idea why, or what was going to happen. And when he said something about putting cuffs on me…to be honest, I just completely froze up. I don't think there was a clear thought in my head."

There was in Griff's. The penalty for murdering the sheriff just might have been worth it if Conner had dared put cuffs on those fragile wrists.

"Griff—the sirens this morning—there was a fire in the library."

"I heard."

"The fire was in the back room. You know, the research and records room? Like where they keep old newspaper records."

"I heard."

"It keeps zinging in my mind. That those would have included newspaper records from the time my dad and mom died. *Those* records."

He shot her a quick look. "You're saying that's the reason for the fire?"

"Oh, no. I'm not saying anything. I don't understand a single thing that's happened since I got here. It just seems there's a growing association to me and these fires." She sighed. "The sheriff wants me to leave town."

And that was another thing that made no sense to Griff. If Conner thought Lily was guilty of these arson events, he should be insisting she stay and be investigated. If he thought she was innocent, there wasn't a reason on the planet why Conner should be pushing her out.

"Griff." Her voice changed tone. The damsel in distress had recovered. She was studying him, staring at him as if she had some kind of laser access into his brain. "You're gripping that steering wheel hard enough to break it off."

"Not really. I was just thinking."

She didn't buy that. "You know," she said gently, "there's nothing wrong with letting out a little anger. Some people have a bigger temper than others. It's not a bad thing. It's only bad if the person does something inappropriate with their temper."

He shot her a serious glower. "I *do not* have a temper."

"You've got a huge one," she informed him. "But you don't use it against people. Or to hurt people. So I think you should just consider accepting it. Some things are always going to push your buttons—like when you don't have the power to control a problem. There's no easy answer for stuff like that, I realize, but you don't have to pretend you don't feel ticked off."

He didn't respond, but he was thinking plenty. Sleep with a woman and what did you get? Mouth. Nonstop. And fear. Damn it, he'd nearly had a heart attack when he heard the fire truck siren in the wee hours of the morning. If she'd stayed in bed with him where she belonged, none of it would have mattered. But she hadn't. She hadn't been where he could see her, touch her. Make sure she was safe.

If that wasn't rational thinking, he didn't remotely care.

"Griff? Um…where are you driving?"

"Debbie's Diner. First off, you need breakfast."

"I couldn't eat a single thing—"

"And second, you need to be into a nice, public place, where people can see you. Instead of people talking about you, you can get in there and talk about them. To them. Out in the open."

"I couldn't eat anything. And I couldn't do that."

"Why?"

"Because…come on, Griff. Instead of making friends, I seem to have done nothing but make enemies here. It's not as if I'm still in middle school, worried about being popular. But sheesh, it's gotten unnerving, feeling so unwanted in town, so judged, when no one even knows me."

"Exactly. I don't know who started all this fire-setter talk, but it's obvious how to stop it. Spend a few seconds with anybody, and they'll realize you're beautiful and warm and smart and good to the bone."

"Huh?"

"Just work with me on this, sugar."

The diner's parking lot was crowded—no surprise, when town news and gossip was running this juicy. But that was the point, Griff thought grimly. It was time to get active. Sitting on the sidelines and watching problems from a distance was the complete worst.

"I can't," she repeated for the fourth time, as he herded her toward the door.

He knew it was hard for her to walk in. And the moment she was spotted in the doorway, talk stopped faster than a switch turned off. The sick look of hurt on her face made him feel a little tense all over again. But sometimes there was only one way to get out a splinter, and that was to just go in there and get the needle part over with.

For a woman who wasn't hungry, she ate two bowls of Griff's Secret—and that was before she even looked at the menu for breakfast food. Debbie was no fool. She greeted them in her typical loud, brassy voice, seated them in plain view, and took care of them herself.

As he'd expected, that was the last time they had two seconds alone. The tall, gray-haired Margo ambled over with a mug in her hand. Being his insurance agent, it would have been odd if she hadn't stopped to say hello, so it was easy to get a conversation going about the fires with her. And so it went. Manuel Brock often had breakfast at the diner; he paused at their table en route to paying his bill. Jason's father—who Griff never had any use for—thought he was a big shot, and put in that he knew who the arsonist was "but he wasn't telling". Louella's second cousin was having breakfast with a lady friend, both wearing rhinestones and sequins on their Vegas-trip sweatshirts. It went on and on....

All of them looked at Lily, even if they aimed conversation at Griff. Some of the older ones mentioned that they'd known her mom or her dad. Some brought up the "old days", when the mill was the major source of employment in town. Someone's sister's mother's cousin's current girlfriend saw her at the library yesterday, saw old man Renbarcker, too. In the way of Southern conversations, cousins four or five times removed were still considered kin, even if they'd been divorced nine thousand times and there was no blood relationship whatsoever. Griff never could keep track of all that, but this morning that wasn't the point.

The point was getting Lily in public. It wasn't so easy to talk about someone, once you'd met them. And if they couldn't see Lily was the most innocent, decent human being they'd ever met, Griff figured they had to be too dumb to waste time on, anyway.

Over the next two hours, his lover—the one who was too nauseous to eat—finished off two dishes of ice cream, a farmer's omelet with all the extras, three cups

of coffee and a brownie. Debbie was trying to hand her
a lunch menu when Griff stood up.

"All right, all right," she said, once they were outside
and aiming for his car. "I admit it. You were right. That
was a good thing to do."

"Of course I was right." He glanced down the street
toward his store, and felt a new stab in the gut, looking
at the burned-out mess. It was fixable. Material things
didn't matter. Still, it hurt. Normally, there'd be a swarm
of kids hanging out there by now—kids who often had
no place to go.

As they walked to the car, he hooked an arm around
Lily's neck, inhaled the scent and touch of her. In the
diner, he hadn't wanted to overdo contact. He wanted to
show the town that they had a connection, that he was
on her side. But to overly let the gossips believe they
were lovers wasn't necessarily the best thing for Lily.
He liked having a bad-boy reputation, but didn't want
her tainted by it. Now, though, that long stretch of not
touching caught up with him.

"After all that food, you want to come home to my
place and catch a nap?"

She looked up at him. "It's not napping on your
mind."

"It is too."

"You lie."

"That's relevant how?"

"It's not. You can lie to me all you want, Griff. I like
it. I especially like it when you're trying to get away with
something. But for a few hours...I'm guessing you have
stuff you need to do in the middle of the day. And I want

to hit the newspaper office, to see if I can track down records of what was going on the year of the fire."

"I'll go with you."

"Does that sound like a thrilling way to spend an afternoon? Pouring over old newsprint? No. You have serious things to do. You've got a clean-up plan to put together, you've got your other work, you've still got ice cream equipment that needs some kind of resolution, you—"

"I don't care about any of that."

She sighed, put her slim hand on his chest. Just like that, he felt the electric connection, the pulse between them, the beat he'd never imagined before. "Griff—go do your life. We can meet up at dinner if you want."

"I'm not—"

"You're worried something's going to happen to me. It's not. Think about it. No one's targeted me. These fires may be somehow *about* me, but no one has actually tried to harm me in any way. I'll be perfectly safe."

He didn't like her ability to read his mind, to draw conclusions without his permission. He also couldn't deny her logic—and it was true he had five million things that needed to get done. At the newspaper office, she'd be around other people.

So he agreed, said he'd pick her up for dinner around seven at the B and B. That was where he dropped her now, so she could get her car. But when he drove off, he felt an uneasy itch, like the nag of a mosquito bite.

No one *had* tried to harm her. But he was afraid someone *would*—because all these fires had to be leading up to something. Unless someone figured out what it was, Lily wasn't safe. He knew it in his head and his heart both.

The Pecan Valley Herald was located just outside of town, sandwiched between peach orchards flanking the east side, and a pre-loved car dealership stretching out to the west. When Lily pulled open the door, she was greeted by a blast of fabulously cold air and a gum-chewing receptionist.

The redhead took one look at her, said, "Bridal or Engagement announcements, down the hall to the left."

"No, I—"

"Classified straight through that door."

It took a while for the redhead to run down her list, they simply asked for "past newspaper history." No one had apparently asked that before, because the young woman looked confounded, but eventually she pushed some buttons and a middle-aged man showed up.

"You're Lily Campbell?" he asked.

Timothy was a sweetheart, disguised in too-short pants and white socks and a zealous comb-over. The reference room was *his,* his source of power, his love. "I'm afraid a lot of the old stuff is still on microfiche. I've been computerizing since I got here, but that's only been three years, and you should have seen the place then. So. You think you want to go through two years of papers?"

"Yes." She told him her goal, which was to track the phrase in the investigative report referring to her parents' fire being "nothing like the other arson events". She just wanted to see what those other fires were about. She realized it was grasping for some mighty slim straws, but it was one of the few things she hadn't tried pursuing before.

"You know how long it's going to take you to read two years' worth of copy?" Timothy asked her.

"I figure…a while."

He sighed. "You can't smoke or eat in here. But that far door, that leads to a restroom, a minikitchen—the coffee pot's usually on—and a back door, if you want to get out in the fresh air."

"There's fresh air in Georgia in the summer?" she asked incredulously.

He looked blank, then chuckled. "I can come back and help you if I get more projects done, but I'm behind. Still, just yell out my name if you want me."

"Thanks, Timothy."

She'd never seen microfiche before. The method was prehistoric as far as she could tell, but it was a way to scroll through page after page of every newspaper edition. *The Pecan Valley Herald* was hardly a big paper, but like in all small towns, it covered every wedding, every funeral, every achievement of every child, every reunion, every recipe…on and on. And on.

The minutes started to add up. Then the hours. Lily felt her neck creaking, her wrist whining from the constant scrolling motion. The monitor was ancient, with no resolution and blurry print. The chair would have fit any fanny that was square. Hers wasn't.

She took a potty break, took another break to stand

at the sink in the employees' room, gulping down two tall glasses of water. She thought blissfully of last night's lovemaking with Griff. Who knew? Who knew she could be wicked? That she could actually throw off her good-girl chains and just, well, go for it?

Who knew she could fall crazy in love? Inappropriately in love? Maybe irrevocably in love, so fast, and with such a wrong guy in the wrong place?

She hiked back to the godawful chair and parked there again. Thinking of Griff wasn't going to solve anything. She had to concentrate on other kinds of fires.

And over the next hour she found several. An old farmhouse: electrical fire. A lightning strike at a trailer park. A divorcing couple who set fire to each other's stuff.

But then she found pay dirt. At least sort of.

Thirteen months before her parents' fire, there'd been an arson event in the high school. The school locker of a junior, a boy named Billy Webb, had been doused with gasoline. No one could pin down a culprit, but Billy claimed his ex-girlfriend was "real, real mad" at him. The girl friend wasn't named in the article, but Sheriff Conner and the school principal were both reported to be doing an extensive investigation.

Then, seven months before her parents' fire, another arson-type fire was reported—this one also targeted a teenage boy. John Thornton had been a high school senior that fall. The day after the Homecoming Dance, someone heaped a pile of rags in the trunk of his fourteen-year-old Grand Am, sprayed it with gasoline and struck a match. Sheriff Conner and the school principal were again quoted. Both said they were looking into the "coincidence" of two fires targeting young men in the high school. No motive was found. No evidence was found.

A letter to the editor was picked up that "someone" should look into what girls these boys had been seeing, since the boys weren't culprits—the boys were the ones who were being targeted. A flurry of letters followed, all from parents of boys worried about their sons. Worried about the school. Worried about the state of education in general.

One parent felt it was all linked to an alien invasion.

Timothy's head showed up in the doorway. "I have to close up fairly soon, Miss Campbell."

"You can kick me out whenever you need. I appreciate your letting me stay here as long as you have."

"It's not a bother. Hardly anyone goes to the trouble of digging into the microfiche records anymore. But I can't leave an outsider alone here. When I have to lock up, I'm afraid you'll have to go."

"Okay."

"In about twenty minutes."

"Okay." She didn't look up. She was getting closer to the time of her parents' fire. Her eyes were burning from staring at the old screen. She tried kicking off a shoe, sitting on one leg. Then kicking off the other shoe, sitting on the other leg.

Then she forgot how tired she was, because she found *another* arson fire. This one took place three months after the Homecoming Dance, just after New Year's. But it wasn't at the school. It was in someone's home….

"Miss Campbell?"

She squinted closer, squirmed closer. It was in an adult's home, but the fire took place in a teenage boy's bedroom. Same setup. A heap of debris and clothing were piled together, this time on the boy's bed, and then soaked with gasoline. The fire took place while the family was out to dinner. The Frasiers—the family involved—were bewildered and upset and terrified. They had insurance, but as Mrs. Frasier was quoted in the article, they'd "never feel safe again." Mr. Frasier said, "There has to be a serial arsonist in town, and nobody is doing a thing about it." The head of the fire department at the time, Rubal Whitney, was fired. A town meeting was called. Herman Conner urged everyone to stay calm, that he was as concerned as everyone else, but the bottom line was a lack of evidence. So far, they had failed to find a link between the fires, if there was one. They needed concrete information. They needed…

"Lily."

Lily whirled around at the sound of Griff's voice. Griff was standing in the doorway with the round-faced Timothy. "Sugar, it's past eight at night. This nice man has kept the place open for you. He could see you were engrossed. But you can come back tomorrow."

"Oh, my heavens. Timothy, I'm so so sorry. I never meant to be a pain. I had no idea how much time had passed."

"It's all right, Miss Campbell. I just started reading a

book. But when Griff came in, I thought it was all right to interrupt you then."

"Of course it was. Oh, I feel terrible to have made you stay so late. It was so inconsiderate, I..." She scrambled to her feet, found one shoe, couldn't find the other. Grabbed her purse, put it down, leaned forward to turn off the machine. Her heap of notes and papers skidded to the floor. "Timothy, I owe you dinner. Or lunch or something. Whatever or whenever you have time. And I promise, if I come back, I'll keep track of the—"

Griff moved in, switched off the machine, scooped up her notes and legal pad, then claimed her hand—tight and snug. "Got room for a few gallons of Griff's Bliss?" he asked Timothy.

Timothy's mouth dropped. "I'd be so grateful. And so would my mother. She loves your ice cream."

"Okay. Maybe I'll send over a sample of a new flavor, too, so your mom can say she was the first one to taste-test it."

Lily wasn't sure how it all turned into a little fiasco, but Timothy, trying to be hospitable, seemed to be tripping all over Griff. And she was carrying all this stuff, bleary-eyed and kind of trip-tired herself. And Griff...well, by the time he bundled her into the car, he started laughing.

"After one of the worst days in the universe," he said, "somehow we found a way to laugh, didn't we?"

She leaned back in the seat. "It's a miracle."

"Nah," he said. "It's just being together. Now let's hear it for everything you've been doing."

She sobered immediately. "You won't believe what I discovered," she said.

"Good stuff?"

"No. Scary stuff. And I'm getting darned tired of finding out scary stuff. You know a place called Silver Ridge?"

He shot her an odd look. "Sure."

"Could we go there?"

Chapter 9

Over a fast dinner of burgers off the grill, Lily relayed all the new information she'd discovered to Griff. The three different teenage boys targeted by arson. The escalating damage of the fires. The original label of vandalism, then arson, then serial arson. And although gasoline was a common accelerant, its repeated use in those arson incidents made up part of the pattern.

"The investigation report covering our fire said there was no link found to those other arson events. But what if there *was* a link, Griff?"

"Like what? There was no teenage boy in your house."

"I know that. But the place next to us was for sale, empty. And the site of our fire was between the two houses."

"But there was no teenage boy in the empty house either," Griff said reasonably.

"Would you quit being so darned logical!" She tried again. "The police never found who caused those other fires."

Griff nodded. "But there were no more arson incidents after your parents' fire."

"Maybe that shocked the arsonist into quitting—because people died in our fire," she speculated. "The question is, why there've been three arson fires *now,* since I came back to town. Or do you think that could be just coincidence?"

"One fire could have been accidental. Three—no way," Griff said grimly.

"That's what I think. That there has to be a reason this started up again. And I still don't understand why the sheriff thinks I should leave town. Maybe that *would* stop the fires, if I disappeared. But he's the sheriff. Doesn't he want to know who's doing this?"

"He's a dad. With kids not far from your age. And he knows how much your family was hurt then. So maybe he doesn't want to see you hurt, sugar."

"I don't want to be hurt either," she grumbled. "But I'm running out of stuff to research. Everything I've found so far seems to verify that my dad never had a single reason to start that fire. But there's no solid proof that the fire wasn't accidental. I don't know if proof like that even exists. Especially after all these years. And you know what?"

She knew it was a child's question, but still he played along. "What?"

"At this point—I'm happy, Griff. I've learned a bunch about my dad. For my sake, for my sisters. That he was a good man. A man of honor. Not a coward. That's all I really needed to know. That he was the man I thought he was."

"And did you need that proof?"

Something in his voice made her look at him, really look. By then they'd finished dinner, popped their few dishes in the dishwasher, and then went out to his car. During the conversation he was driving, and even though the sun was dropping fast, she could see his profile clearly, see the oddly guarded expression when he'd asked that question. "No," she said slowly. "I always knew my dad was a good man. Yes, I wanted the public proof, if I could find it, to clear his name. But I really don't care what anyone ever said about him—I knew what was true in my heart."

"So you trust your heart, do you?"

She kept looking at him. "I do. I have extraordinary judgment with people," she murmured. "Particularly with men."

He let out an amused chuckle. "You don't think you're just a bit on the trusting side?"

"You sound like my sisters—and they're wrong, too. I trust very, very, very rarely. And it takes even more than that for me to trust at a gut level. Which I can prove."

"How's that?"

"I slept with you, didn't I? I picked you to seduce, out of the hoards and hoards of men I could have chosen— seeing as how I'm gorgeous and smart and all that." She figured she'd make him laugh again. Instead he shot her another strange look.

"How could you *not* know that you're gorgeous and smart and 'all that'? Or are all the guys deaf and blind where you live?"

"Aw, that Southern sweet talk is water for a girl's worst thirst."

"What if it isn't sweet talk?"

"Not to distract you from this totally silly conversation, but where on earth *are* we?"

"Where you asked me to take you. I admit I was surprised. But I always try to do what a lady asks."

"*This* is Silver Ridge?"

"Well—we'll get to Silver Ridge, sugar. It's just a little complicated. Now, I brought bug spray. And we're just following this short trail to the boat. I want you to keep your hands and feet in the boat at all times. There are gators and snakes in the water."

"*What?* Wait a minute. Wait, wait, wait. *Wait!* This isn't what I signed up for…." She galloped after him, but it didn't do any good.

"Too late to change your mind now. There's a time when you can always tell a man no, sugar. But this isn't about sex. And why ever you thought you wanted to come here, at this point you're getting your money's worth. I guarantee it."

"Wait. Wait…"

After eating, she, knew they were headed for Silver Ridge, where she'd asked to go. But she was whipped after the emotional and physical day. She hadn't paid any attention to their outside surroundings. In the car, she'd looked at Griff, only at Griff. Being with him had lifted her spirits and her heart like nothing else possibly could have. Somehow, he made her feel like a pure female— with an absolutely pure male.

His clothes certainly didn't define him. He was just wearing chinos, sandals, a polo; his hair was ruffled up and his chin had the day's shadow of a beard. Another guy would have looked casual. Griff somehow managed to look not quite respectable at the same time. And sexy. Damn man was always sexy. Trouble from head to toe, from his eyes to his butt to the shape of his hands.

If she had to sin, Lily thought, she was so glad it was him. There was no point in doing something halfway. Since she'd fallen off the Good Girl Wagon, she could at least fall the whole huge distance to a man as compellingly wrong for her as Griff.

But this…

She was still following him, but not happily. She'd had the sense in the car that he was testing her in some odd way; but whatever that test was, she decided she was willing to fail it. This was too darned scary.

Night hadn't completely fallen on the jagged path from the cliff to the water. Minutes of sunset were still left, that time when the sky was a violent purple, a ruby red, a deepening sapphire. In another ten minutes, she wouldn't be able to see the ghastly scene in front of her.

The water had that black, murky stillness of a swamp in a horror movie, backdropped by big old oaks and their bearded moss. Invisible things in the shadows made sounds, hungry sounds, scary sounds. The "boat" he motioned her toward looked like a raft. An inadequate raft. It looked as if someone had glued a bunch of boards together, makeshift fashion, creating a tiny patio with a white vinyl bench and seat, with a little box table nailed in the middle.

"We're not going on that, are we?"

"Uh-huh."

"But snakes could climb up on that. Alligators. There could be leeches in that water. Or the moss could strangle us. We could sink. It doesn't have any sides. It doesn't have any motor—"

"Hey, don't be blaming me for this deal. This wasn't my idea. It was yours. This is the way to Silver Ridge."

"Griff, honestly, couldn't you afford a little better boat?"

"This one's ideal for where we're going. Pretty much a pole raft is the only way to navigate a shallow swamp. It's not something I do very often, but for this trip, it's perfect for what you want to see."

"Perfect?" She said the word as if testing it, then shook her head. "Bad things are going to try and grab us in the dark," she said ominously.

"Uh-huh. It's going to be very scary. Very dangerous. Probably the riskiest thing you've done in your whole life."

"Hey. Don't make fun of a woman when she's busy being a major wimp."

But Lily had to stop talking. She was having too much fun. It was like living out the old Kathryn Hepburn *African Queen* fantasy—not that Lily wanted any experience with leeches—but the swampy darkness and sounds and moss-draped trees were impossibly romantic. Possibly, Griff already realized she was into that kind of corniness, because she'd leapt onto the raft without prompting, and immediately took up the Princess Position, lounging on the cushions. Griff picked up the long pole.

"So—where are we shoving off to, cap'n?"

With a grin, Griff motioned into the darkness. "We're just hugging the shore, for about ten minutes. You can take a turn steering if you want."

"I won't tip us over?"

"There's only about a foot of water. And it's warm. Not a good place to swim—the bottom's too yucky—but it won't kill us if we get wet."

"Are you going to serve me champagne and grapes?"

"Nope, but there's a cold chest in that box. Bottles of water if you're thirsty. And emergency chocolate."

"Chocolate is a basic food group. It's always an emergency," she informed him. She'd never have believed it—that the day's stresses—the week's stresses—seemed to ease away. She didn't stop thinking about fires and mysteries and frustrations. It was just…this was definitely an hour off.

An hour completely free.

An owl whooed its dusty call. The rich smells of moss and loamy earth and vegetation hit her nose like an exotic perfume. Frogs burped in unison from the shoreline, where grasses rustled and vines climbed the increasingly steep bank. Mist ribboned between trees, danced in the shadows.

On the left, rock increasingly dominated the landscape.

She didn't know if the stone was limestone or granite, but it was almost stark white in darkness, and where the moonlight hit it, silver.

"So...this is Silver Ridge." She couldn't stop looking. The moonlight on the rock was darned near breathtaking, as shiny silver as a jeweler's treasure.

"Yeah." Griff locked the pole, came over and sank to the deck beside her. "As far as I can tell, it's been the lover's lane here for centuries. Kids park on top of the ridge. Or boat in, like we're doing. There's one deep spot, just off the cliff edge—the kids have used it as a swimming hole for years. There's an underground spring there, keeps the water cool and clean. Parents have forbid kids from coming here, but it never does any good. On a weekend night—or a prom night—they could clean up selling tickets to get a parking spot on top of the ridge."

But not tonight. There was no one here this night. But them.

Griff raised a hand, sifted his fingers idly through her hair. His touch was infinitely light, as tender as softness. His eyes found hers in the darkness.

"I forgot why we're here," she murmured.

"Above. On top of the ridge. This was where one of the arson fires were set, long ago. You wanted to see where it was."

"A lovers' lane." She knew. Not the kind of *knew* where she could prove it in a court of law, but all the things she'd learned and read came together with that single snap. "It was a girl who set the fires back then. A girl scorned. Hurt by some boy she thought she liked. Or *boys,* in the plural."

"That's how I'd see it, from the stuff you uncovered."

"Arsonists are more commonly male." Lily remembered reading that.

"Maybe those are the statistics. But the first fire was in a boy's locker, then a boy's bedroom, then a lover's lane site. And since the boys were all the victims, it just seems like it had to be a girl."

"A girl who felt hurt. Or humiliated. Or angry."

"Or all three. A girl who needed some kind of revenge."

The more Griff rubbed her scalp, combing fingers into her hair, the more Lily was afraid she'd fall into some drugged bliss state. It's not as if she was normally a sensualist. She was just a sucker for a head rub, and it'd been years since anyone had given her one. "You think it's the same girl who's been setting the fires this week?"

"I don't know. But two plus two usually equals four. I've been thinking how the rest of it adds up. Just supposition. But the three fires in the past weren't set to deliberately hurt any of those boys. Just to hurt property. To let those boys know she wasn't happy with their behavior. And the three fires since you've been home—they have to be about you. Because you're the only link. But no one's tried to hurt you specifically. It seems like an echo. She's telling you that she's not happy with your behavior. That you're here. Looking into this."

"Griff."

"What?"

"I think your reasoning is brilliant. And scary. But I can't think about this anymore. Not right now."

"How come?"

"You know how come." But she didn't move. And his fingers kept up that magic scalp massage. The moon and the sweet, rich smells and barely rocking raft and Griff, his closeness, all seemed to come together like wine. Too much wine. Way, way too much wine.

"I have this feeling…that you're easy, Lily."

"I am. I am."

"You don't seem impressed by money. I can't see you lusting after jewels. But I just don't know about the strength of your character—when you're so willing to cave for a little scalp rub."

She needed to correct one item there. "Hey, I like jewels. Or I'm sure I could get into jewels, if I just had the chance."

"So on a set of scales, jewels at one end, and a scalp rub on the other…"

"All right, all right, I admit it. Nothing compares to a scalp rub. But in general, there's plenty of greed and selfishness and stuff like that in my character."

"I think we should encourage those things." Even though the white boat cushion was long and narrow, he managed to twist her on her stomach without even nominally rocking the boat—conceivably because she was limper than noodles and already completely pliable. His hands chased up her tee, unhooked her bra. She considered expressing a little outrage—or at least surprise—but by then he was already rubbing and kneading and stroking her back.

It wasn't her fault that she caved. How awful could a day be? Being hauled to the police department. Being almost arrested. Feeling responsible for the fire in the library. Feeling responsible for the fire at Griff's. Not even knowing why she was feeling responsible. And then uncovering all that messy past stuff at the newspaper office—good information, good clues, but still nothing substantial enough to change the past or present. On top of which, Griff's dragging her into the diner that morning had been a stomach-clencher. Yes, people talked to her, but initially they'd looked at her with such suspicion, it had felt like wearing a red stripe in her hair. No one looked at her as if they saw *her*. They just saw the red stripe.

And Griff…damn the man, but he was turning into her vice. The best vice she'd ever taken up. She never thought she could do it—throw everything to the wind for one man, one wild fling of irresponsible sex, and not feel a single ounce of guilt. This was so right that she just couldn't care. He was so right for her heart, for her soul, for her life at this moment, that nothing else could possibly matter more.

He kneaded and rubbed and stroked, her neck, scalp, down the slope of her spine, pushing her shorts down to just the swell of her fanny, where he could rub the very small of her back. "You're tense," he murmured. "Pecan Valley hasn't exactly been a vacation for you, has it?"

He didn't mean it as a question. Didn't mean for her to answer. But if he thought she was tense because of her personal problems, she needed to correct that notion immediately.

She was tense, all right.

Because of him.

For him.

She twisted beneath him, setting the raft on a wild rock, startling the vulnerable shine in Griff's eyes. Oh yeah, she wasn't the only one who needed love. She suspected he'd never had a shortage of offers for sex. But love wasn't the same thing at all.

She found his mouth, took it. It wasn't a moment of pleasure she wanted to offer him—but a moment of risk. It was her turn to rub and knead and stroke. Her hands stole under his shirt, pushed up the fabric, not caring that it bunched, not caring that her knees and elbows seemed to be in the wrong place.

"Hey, sugar…" His voice was lazy as molasses, but his eyes weren't. His gaze was all fire and heat, his skin already glazed, his intent as explosive as any accelerant could possibly be. "You started things last time. Don't you think we should take turns?"

"No."

"No?" The hint of a smile in his voice. "Well… we could argue about it. I can't think of a more fun argument. But this time, this night, I just can't let you win, Lily, I'm sorry."

He wasn't sorry. He wasn't the least bit sorry. What he knew and what she knew was a little like comparing candlelight to a forest fire. She was a quick learner, but it was hard to catch up with a guy who'd been around as many blocks as he had. And he was so darned fast.

Clothes were pushed and pulled and yanked free.

Some, she feared, went into the water. For sure, a shoe did.

Moonlight caught the gleam of his hair, the glisten of his skin…the need in his face, in his heart. Maybe he thought this was about seduction. But she closed her eyes and just…gave.

Everything she had.

His tongue on her breast, his palm sliding down into her panties, into her…the way he clenched that contact. He knew it would ignite her. He knew.

But she knew a few things, too. She knew as much about loneliness as he did. She knew intimately about traveling life solo, about a heart too damaged to risk any more losses, about always that need, that hunger, that hole deep down that never got filled. It wasn't something she shared with anyone else. It wasn't something she could even explain. But she knew Griff at some level, knew his heart at some level. Knew…

Knew nothing. Except to touch and give and lay her wants bare. They slid against each other, skin slick, lips wet, need trembling with more and more ferocity raging between both of them. She used her hands as an accelerant, finding a way to stroke him, to tease the long, firm length of him…until he let out of a growl of frustration. Such a growl that she had to laugh.

She quit laughing when he plunged inside her. Her eyes popped open, met his, matched his. She wound her legs up and tight on his hips, felt him scooch her even higher, felt him driving, driving, driving into her like a lion possessing his mate. He'd have hurt her, except he couldn't. She was wet, willing, encouraging the wildness, encouraging him to let go, to be. With her. All he was.

He came on a long guttural groan that echoed her own fierce cry. The tight pulsing explosions seemed to go on and on, pleasure that stole both her breath and her heart.

Silence followed that symphony of sensation. He eased his weight off her, but then just pulled her close. She practiced trying to breathe normally, but it was tough, with his fingers softly threading through her hair, his gaze on her face as if she were the sun and the moon and then some.

Eventually frogs got around to burping again. Owls restarted their hoot thing. Maybe those sounds had been happening before, but she hadn't heard them. She hadn't heard or seen anything but Griff.

"We can't ever do this again," she murmured regretfully.

His brow raised. "Hmm. I could have sworn you were having a good time a few moments ago."

"Oh. I was. But that's just the thing. We keep doing this, you'll have permanently ruined me for anyone else. Before you, I was perfectly happy thinking that making love was a nice thing to share between two people who really, really care about each other."

His eyebrows raised again. "And now you don't think that?"

"Of course not. You're ruining me, like I said. I didn't know it could be…you know. Insane. Crazy. Wanting so much you hurt. Needing so much you can't breathe.

Flying over the moon so high you don't need wings. That kind of thing."

"All right. If you're willing to get into that deep, dark confession territory—I have to admit, I've always been fond of sex."

"No kidding?"

He tugged her hair. Gently. "But I can't say I've ever experienced what we've been doing. The incendiary thing. The starting a fire that turns into an explosive, hot, uncontrollable thing. The wanting you beyond being able to think or speak or even care if the rest of the world were falling in."

"See what I was saying? We just can't do this again. It's too dangerous."

"You don't think there's any other answer?"

"Well...maybe we could just stay here. Right here. On this raft. Forever."

She didn't mean any of it of course, because she was a practical, serious, responsible person, always had been, always would be. But just then...she meant every word. She loved the banter. Loved the roll of his voice, the hush of it, the promise of it. She loved his tenderness. Who knew? That a man so full of the devil could have that much tenderness? Could show it?

Could share it.

She started to say something—then heard the buzz, saw the mosquito, and fast, slapped Griff's shoulder.

"Uh-oh. Is the love affair over already?" he complained.

"I was helping you. I killed the mosquito before it got you."

"Well, shoot. I thought we were both pretty well coated up with bug spray—but I suspect if they're starting to land, we'd better get out of here."

"Are you going to let me pole back?"

"Sugar, I'd let you do anything you wanted, anything you asked for. Just try me."

"Oh, good. Because I was rethinking that jewelry business. I've never been that fond of diamonds, but I do like amethysts. All the colors of amethyst, purples and greens, the whole lot. Oh. And opals. I've never seen an opal I didn't lust after. Rings, earrings, necklaces, bracelets…" He may or may not have noticed that she never wore jewelry, but roleplaying a greedy golddigger kept him chuckling as she poled them back.

It was fun. Figuring out how to make the raft move via the pole took a certain rhythm to figure out, but then it was like…dancing. Gliding into the darkness, with the white-silver ridge behind them, and the snowy moon speckling light through the leaves.

For tonight, Griff had done the impossible—made her forget fears and worries, fires and frauds. Not completely. But somehow, when she was with Griff, she believed everything would ultimately come out all right.

If that belief was irrational, she didn't care.

When they reached shore, he tied up the raft, grabbed the armload of gear he'd brought, and still managed to find a hand to hold hers, climbing back up to the car. "You're coming home with me tonight."

He didn't phrase it like a question, but she answered it that way. "Not a good idea."

"Why."

"Because…I need fresh clothes. I don't have anything but what I'm wearing."

"I've got a shirt you can put on. And a washer and dryer just like everyone else."

"Louella will worry if I don't come home. The darned woman waits up."

"So you can phone her."

"I can't phone her! Then she'll know I'm sleeping with you!"

"Ah. The puritan streak surfaces. But we can still solve that. *I'll* phone her and tell her some lie. Like that you fell asleep while we were watching a Walt Disney movie, so I just let you crash on my couch." He paused, apparently saw the "no" was still on her face. "Okay, sugar. Now what's the real reason you don't want to sleep over?"

"Because." She climbed into the car seat, curled up, and strapped on the seat belt with a major yawn.

When he climbed in the other side, he reached over, kissed her, turned the key, and then resumed their mature conversation. "Because why?"

"Do I have to have a reason? Can't a girl just say no?"

"Of course you can. But I won't stop badgering you until you give me one."

"Come on, Griff. The first time I met you, I told you to stay away from me. People love you here. And you've been standing by me, which I appreciate. But I don't want you hurt by being with me. By being associated with me."

He shot out on the highway. "I had a feeling it was a really dumb reason like that."

"It's not dumb."

"*You're* not dumb. You're plenty smart. But that *is* a dumb reason. We're in the South, sugar. A few are still concerned about who won the War of Aggression. But even if we don't talk about it, grown-ups are generally allowed to be in love. To love. And if anyone had a problem with that, I wouldn't want to know them. Or for you to waste your time on them. And—"

"And what?"

"And if you come home with me, we can take a shower together. You saw my shower room. It has seats. You can choose pulsing spray or rain or jets or any other speed of water you want. Any temperature you want. I've got towels thicker than your finger—"

"Stop." She put her hand over her ears. "I can't stand this level of temptation."

"Good," he murmured and took her home.

Chapter 10

Griff knew what a long day she'd had. As he ushered her inside, his thought was a soothing soaker for them both, after which he'd pour her into bed.

That wasn't his preferred plan. Ideally he'd make love to her again—maybe twice. His body was inspired to replicate the extraordinary experience on the raft—on a comfortable mattress. But that was pretty damned selfish. There was always the morning.

And the next morning.

And the next morning after that.

"Griff…" She yawned as she stumbled in behind him. "I see the blinking light on your machine. You've got messages."

"They'll wait." He switched on a living room lamp, only to illuminate their path back to his room. He'd turned off his cell, knew she'd turned off hers for a few hours that evening. Surely they were safe from any more emergencies or catastrophes for a few hours. He needed that time with her.

It was still rattling in his head—an awareness that all the sweet talk after making love hadn't been sweet talk. Not for him. He was hooked.

He'd never been hooked. In lust, a million times. In crush, more than a million. In love. Real love. Never.

The sensation was damn near terrorizing.

Abruptly, he heard her shriek coming from down the hall, and had to grin.

"Come on. You've seen the bathroom before."

"I wouldn't care if I'd seen it a dozen times. That's not the point! The point is that I'm living with you forever! That's it! Don't argue with me! Nothing and no one will ever make me leave you!"

"Yeah, yeah. *Now* you talk big. But the first time I snore you'll probably run for the hills." He pushed off shoes, switched on the bedside lamp, pulled off his shirt—but she wasn't paying any attention to him.

She was still shrieking and crowing from his bathroom. "This is *sinful*. You should be ashamed! Talk about sybaritic. Talk about—"

"Don't be so shy. Tell me what you really think." The bedroom, truth to tell, wasn't much. He never spent much time there. The mattress was the best money could buy, the sheets high quality, but otherwise, it was just a big room that did a good job of shutting out noise and distractions. Back when he'd been a serious insomniac.

That had been part of his motivation for the fancy shower. De-tensing wasn't easy for him. Everyone thought he was a low-key guy—everyone except Lily, anyway. The reality was that he used to walk the floor at nights, so tired he couldn't think, yet still unable to sleep. He told her about that.

"Sounds like pretty serious insomnia," she said.

"It was. One time, I went three days without sleep. I started to get downright weird."

"Of course you did."

He frowned, unsure how she'd sort of manipulated things. He'd barely stepped in the bathroom before she was pulling off his shirt, peeling down his shirt, looking up at him with a grin that…well, hell. Obviously he was aroused again. He could have nailed railroad spikes with the hammer strength of his hard-on. That was her doing. He was *trying* to be good.

She'd raved about his bathroom before, but he figured she might be laying it on thick because she was Lily, and she knew he loved the damned room. The core structure was white marble and lapis—nice, but the big to-do was the shower room. The glass wall overlooked the ravine. It was fun as hell, being naked, feeling like you were in the open. Every bird in the county could see you—maybe raccoons, if they could climb high enough. But there were no houses or humans with that kind of visibility.

The other three walls of the shower were redwood, as were the long, layout benches. The shower had a double step-down, so you could soak feet, or sit in waist-high water…or you could just stand there and do the shower thing, choose either a deluge or tropic storm or spring rain, depending on the force of water you wanted.

As far as he could tell, Lily wanted it all. Just stood

there and lapped it all in like a sea nymph. He shampooed her hair, because she was such a sucker for a head rub. From the suds to the sluice of water to the slick textures of soap and silky skin, he saw the building laughter in her eyes. That natural sensuality coming out of hiding. That come-on in her expression, as if all inhibitions had been stripped away, locked out of this room—*their* room—their moment together.

And it was light in here, not dark, like on the raft. He could run his hands down—*walk* his hands down—all the slopes and valleys at a nice, slow pace. Her breasts had an extra tightness. "Lumpy," she whispered.

He understood. She was warning him that she was tender, probably pre-period tender. He was more than happy to be careful, infinitely careful. He could have played on her skin all night. Cartwheels. Sonatas. Poetry. Rock and roll. Art. He wanted to drink her in in every which way….

Until out of the blue, he noticed her suddenly trembling.

"Hey? You cold?"

"No. No." She lifted her head. Smiled. He saw the terror in her eyes. "I know what you're doing," she said.

Her voice was brave.

"Yeah?"

She rushed on. "Both of us have been doing a lot of play talk. Pretending like we have a relationship. But you live here, Griff, and I don't. I can't even imagine coming back here to live. And I just want to be sure you know—I'm happy playing. I never expected more."

"No?" He murmured, and started switching off the jets, the faucets. She sounded as sure as a leaf in the wind.

"Absolutely not," she promised him. "I'm happy with us. Just as we are."

That chin was tilted up, but she still couldn't hide that crack in her voice.

He reached for a towel—one of those bigger-than-a-blanket towels, so it was easy to get her immediately covered and warmer. He rubbed her dry, thinking this was the best job he'd had in a long time.

"I don't want more," she said. "You don't have to worry. This is perfect just as it is."

"Uh-huh." It was hard to buy the deal she was selling him. Lily was a player like Bambi was a wrestler. He'd known it from the start. She wasn't a one-shot deal. An affair. A wonderful—but forgettable—lover.

She was unforgettable even before he'd taken her to bed.

For a man who'd resisted all efforts to be tied down—who had never allowed himself to believe in permanence, who didn't believe himself capable of caring that much—she was shaking his timbers. And he didn't like it.

Still, if he was stuck suffering the terrors of falling in love, he wasn't the only one going down.

"Hey," she murmured. "I'm smothering."

When he wrapped her up in the big towel, her face had gotten accidentally covered. "I will never," he promised, "smother you." He laid her down on the bed, switched off the light, then dove down beside her. He pulled back the towel edge just to see her face.

A wicked smile was waiting for him. Her eyes were dark with desire, with boldness. Some of that bravado was still hovering in her trembling mouth when he dipped down and took it. In the process of that kiss, he discovered that his own damn mouth was trembling, too.

"Lily," he whispered, and started to say something else—when the telephone rang.

The cell phones had been turned off, and the ringer wasn't from his landline. The chime was from the private cell he kept on the dresser, an emergency number that only a handful of people had.

Lily saw his expression change. "Go," she said.

"I have to answer it."

She just nodded, lifted up on her elbows as he vaulted across the room and grabbed the phone.

He didn't know ahead which kid was calling, just that it was a kid. Jason's voice could sound as if he were one hundred and ten years old or four. This was a small child's voice. "You said I could call if I ever really had trouble."

"You know you can. Where are you?"

"The road into Shanty Creek. The woods left of the entrance road there." A pause. "The bugs are pretty bad. I just wondered if—"

"I'll be there. Take me less than ten." He filled Lily in while he yanked on pants, a tee, pushed on sandals, grabbed his car keys.

"Do you want me to go back to Louella's?"

"No."

"Do you want me to make up a bed, that kind of thing…?"

He should have known she'd get the picture.

Less than a half hour later, he was bringing Jason into the house. The boy had been in worse shape. There were no broken bones this time, no burns. But the right eye was almost swollen shut, and he'd taken a kick to the kidneys that made him wince when he walked. Every mosquito in the county had nailed him, and his face had that look—that no one's gonna reach me look—that Griff had seen before, but Lily sure as hell hadn't.

She'd pulled on a T-shirt of his, a pair of his shorts, somehow found some string, tied it into a belt to hold up the crazy outfit. His washing machine was running. A first-aid kit sat open on the counter. She took one look at Jason, sucked in a breath, lifted frantic eyes to him—and then just moved.

"Well, if you aren't a complete mess," she murmured gently. "Let's get you cleaned up and some ice on that eye. You go bury yourself in mud, did you? You hungry, honey?"

Jason didn't want to look at her, didn't want to talk to her, clearly didn't expect anyone to be there but Griff.

Griff could see she was handling him. She kept up a steady patter of gentle talk, which enabled him to do what he needed to immediately do—which was to hit the phone.

He called Sheriff Conner first, woke him up, told him where the boy was. "Nobody getting any sleep this week in the whole durned town," The sheriff grumbled. "You know Lily hasn't left town besides."

"Lily is right here with me."

"Well, at least we know she isn't setting fires. You call Loreen?"

"She's next."

"Need a hospital?"

"Close. But no."

"All right. I'll check with you first thing in the morning."

He called the social worker, Loreen. They'd been through the same routine a half-dozen times before.

The house didn't quiet down until past three in the morning. Lily sat in the spare bedroom until Jason fell asleep. She left a light on, the door open, tiptoed into his bedroom with zombie eyes. His were just as blurry.

"How often does that happen?" she asked. "And what happens to Jason after this?"

He gave her the rundown. He called, told people where Jason was, so there'd be no question. The sheriff would roust Jason's father, coop him up for a few days. It was like a lot of life's problems: everyone knew what should happen, but it wasn't that simple to make "right things" happen in an imperfect world.

"I've gotten Jason out of the house, into foster care before—but so far, he's always found a way to steal back home. He doesn't want to leave his mom and younger brother. So he goes back. The mom'll get counseling. The dad'll get counseling and jail hours. The dad'll be real, real sorry. And it'll happen again. Until Jason's mom leaves the creep. That's the real answer. But so far she's not willing to do it."

"And how did you get involved?"

"Beats me. I'm just trying to sit around and sell a little ice cream."

"Griff."

"What?"

"It's a little late to sell me the lazy bad-boy persona."

He shut his eyes. "He wants me to take him in. But that's not an answer, you know? I know Jason thinks it is. Steve. A couple other kids. But what they really need is more complicated than that. They need a legal system that works for them, that they know how to use. They need to develop enough insight to analyze who to trust, who not to trust. They need to see and believe that good people will stand up for them. They need to believe that life can work, that things can be better, that there are other choices and how to get to them."

He yawned.

"You didn't need this on top of the arson problem, did you?" she murmured, and then, "What is this? We're talking like kids on a sleepover. It's the middle of the night."

"Well, quit talking then, sugar."

"You first."

"I can't go to sleep if you're going to spoon against me like that."

"Oh, yeah you can," she whispered again, and the damn woman—and really, Lily could be mighty annoying sometimes—was right.

That was the last thing he remembered until daylight.

* * *

When Lily awoke, she was burrowed into Griff's shoulder like a squirrel in wintertime. The room was snuggle-cool, all the shades drawn, Griff's warmth the perfect way to open her eyes.

Until she did open her eyes, and unfortunately remembered her life.

She was in a strange bed, wearing nothing at all, in the middle of a town of people who seemed to think she was an arsonist, where trying to clear her father's name had caused unexplained trouble for everyone. On top of which, she was in love with a man she had as much in common with as peanut butter and anchovies.

It was enough to wake up a girl fast.

She sneaked out of bed, tiptoed around to find toothpaste and steal his deodorant, then pulled yesterday's clothes out of the dryer and went in search of a coffeemaker. Griff needed all the sleep he could get, she figured—since being around her seemed to have shortened everyone's sleep in the whole town. Including her own.

She peeked in on Jason, who was also sleeping like the dead, curled up in a fetal position, the light still on, looking very much like a normal, innocent ten-year old…except for the swollen red-and-black eye. Her heart clenched. It wasn't *totally* her fault she'd fallen for Griff. The big faker was exactly that kind of man—the type who'd take in a battered kid, who'd take on the system, who'd pick up a child who wasn't remotely his responsibility in the middle of the night and stand up for him.

She aimed for his kitchen, prowled around. The boys

were going to probably want eggs and a serious breakfast, so she located where various pots and pans and supplies were, then started up his German coffee machine.

While coffee brewed, she dug in her purse for her cell phone, switched it on. Voicemail indicated almost a dozen calls—six of them from Cate. Her oldest sister had probably worked herself into an ulcer by now.

Lily waited until she had the first mug poured, then carried it through the living room, opened a glass door and sank in a chair on the patio. The morning was already lushly warm, but a breeze whisked through the air. More to the point, the boys wouldn't likely hear raised voices from outside, and Cate, even from a thousand miles away, was likely mad enough to rival a symphony in volume. She took a long pull on the coffee, hit redial, and waited for the blast.

"You don't put yourself in dangerous situations, you dimwit. Do you hear me? The three of us—we're not losing each other. Period. If you're in trouble, we're all in trouble, and now we've got a couple of husbands to add to the protection force. You don't just…"

Yada yada. Lily finished the first cup, went back for a second before she got a word in edgewise, and finally slipped in an "I totally love you, Cate." Usually that stopped Cate dead in her tracks, no matter how wild a rant she was on.

And that worked for a while. She filled Cate in on the newspaper records, the teenage girl likely responsible for three of the old arson fires, how or if they could possibly be linked to their parents' fire—and the current arson incidents.

Cate interrupted to ask, "So that teenage girl, she'd be between thirty-five and forty now?"

"Add twenty years to back then. Yes."

But neither of them could seem to conclude more than that. It had been a long time since Lily had been able to coax Cate—or Sophie—to talk about the fire. All three knew what that fire had cost them—fear of loss, grief that never went away, the loss of home and life and everything they knew. None of the three had ever felt safe again.

It was always there, the knowledge that fate could suddenly step in and rip out everything from beneath you.

Lily said, "My plan today is to hit the social service office. I don't know if the social worker is still there who had our case, but it's really bugged me. Why were the three of us separated? Doesn't have anything to do with the fire, I guess—but I want to know how it was decided that we sisters should be split up."

"Good," Cate said thoughtfully. "And then...did you happen to look up the old high school yearbooks?"

Lily frowned, looked into her empty cup, and ambled back to the kitchen with the cell still glued to her ear. "Why?"

"You pinned down a reason for fires. Something we never had before. A girl who was jilted or hurt. The year of the fire—and maybe the year before? So, if she was a teenager, maybe her picture will be in the high school yearbook."

"I can't imagine that I could conceivably recognize anyone."

"Probably not." Cate sighed. "It's just grasping at straws. But even if the faces mean nothing to you, maybe a name will ring a bell. Or something could be familiar."

"Okay. No harm in trying." She heard a door open, saw Griff emerge from the hall, his hair sleep-tousled, his chin beard-bristly. Barefoot, wearing nothing but cutoffs, she thought he looked downright edible.

"Then get out, Lily. I mean it. I admit, I'm glad you went there. Sophie is, too. You uncovered a bunch of things that we never expected to know, and we all wanted that. But no 'closure' malarkey is worth your being in danger. Cross your *T*s, see if there's anything else to find, but then, for Pete's sake, pack up."

"Hmm." She watched Griff pause in Jason's doorway, peer in, and then make a beeline straight for her. Didn't look right or left, didn't notice the day or the darkening sky or the mess in his kitchen. He pounced. Pressed a kiss tight to the top of her head. Then zoned for the coffee machine.

"Lily, are you listening?"

"Yes."

"You're at his house, aren't you."

"Yes."

"Stop saying 'yes' or I'm flying there as fast as I can buy ticket. How far has it gone?"

"As far as anything in my life," Lily said simply. She hung up. Not intentionally. She saw Griff had filled his mug and had already put it down, was aiming for her again. Without thinking about it, she put down the phone—just in time to lift both her arms. Griff slid right between them, and hooked her into a good-morning kiss. A serious good-morning kiss this time. A life-altering good-morning kiss.

"Hey," he murmured. The light in his eyes was strong enough to burn.

"Hey right back."

"I have an idea."

She laughed, shook her head. "We both have major agendas today. No time for ideas, big guy."

"I'm fast."

"Last I noticed, you were dazzlingly slow. But a far more immediately important agenda issue is walking up beyond you, handsome."

Griff arched an arm, felt even before he saw Jason edge out of the hallway shadows, hustle to take a quick place against his side. Griff gently squeezed a hug, then let him loose. Lily watched him take a long look at the young, battered face.

"We've got some things to take care of, my main man."

"I'm up for anything you are," Jason said, and offered a hesitant smile to Lily.

"You guys aren't going anywhere without a decent breakfast. Don't even try," Lily warned them.

The day's plans were aired over scrambled eggs and guava-jam-covered toast. Griff had running around to do, organizing the cleanup of his shop, a little real work, some ordinary chores. "Jason's hanging with me through that. But after lunch, we're going to make a stop at social services."

"No," Jason said immediately.

"I didn't say you'd be stuck there. I said we're going in there together. Loreen'll take pictures. And you'll go back to your mom's—if your dad's in custody." Griff fielded his dishes to the sink. Jason did the same.

"It sounds like we're going to run some parallel paths," Lily admitted. She was headed back to the B and B first for a change of clothes, then headed for social services herself, to see if there were records from twenty years ago on the disposition of her and her sisters. After that, she wanted to track down high school yearbooks for the two years before the fire.

"At soc services, ask for Loreen. She's sharp, good lady. She'll do you a favor if she can."

They made a tentative plan to catch up predinner, but Lily wasn't taking odds on that happening and told him so. "You've had days since you had a chance to get into your own office here. You need and have to get some time to yourself."

"No, I don't," he argued.

"Well, we'll see." She wanted to be with him—more than he knew. But there was no guessing how long Jason would be with him, and no forecasting how long either of their days would be. "Call my cell if you want to cancel out—or if you have stuff to do and you just want me and Jason to hang out. At least, if that's okay with Jason."

It wasn't quite. She could still see wariness in Jason's eyes. There was only one person the child really trusted, and that was Griff. But he agreed—where Griff didn't. Griff insisted on their catching up via cell several times during the day. And she couldn't escape until she'd agreed to the tyrant's demands.

Naturally though, nothing went as planned.

Chapter 11

It was almost noon before Lily located the old Department of Social Services building. Louella had held her up for the better part of an hour, wanting to gossip, hoping for more information. She'd changed clothes to a sleeveless shift, pale pink and white, as cool as anything she owned, and tried winding her hair with a clip on top of her head. The temperature by the time she returned to her rental car was the usual—hot, wet and steamy.

She'd have made it to the Department of Social Services building a good half hour earlier, if she didn't make a couple wrong turns—and then had to fill up with gas. Finally, though, she located the flat-topped brick building on the far side of the railroad tracks. Once inside, everything got easier. She only had to ask for Loreen.

Griff's contact had chocolate caramel skin, wore a

print dress a size too small for her ample curves, and the tired face of a woman who'd seen it all. "Griff said you might stop. Heaven knows, I've been curious to lay eyes on you. Whole town's talking about you and these fires. Come on back. I'll get us both some sweet tea."

"Oh, I don't need—"

"*I* do. And from everything I've been hearing, you need all the sweet tea and sympathy you can get."

Loreen's office was jammed. File cabinets and desk overflowed with paper. The walls had pictures of missing kids, framed diplomas and credentials, schedules. One corner of the desk was reserved for a pitcher of sweet tea, cold and sweating on a tray with paper cups. "You just missed Griff by two shakes, was in here with the boy. Jason, his daddy's bad to the bone. Got a nice smile, a nice look. It's gonna kill me—and it's gonna kill Griff worse—if the kid ends back in that house again."

"I'm guessing you've tried to rescue him before."

"So many times, I lost count. I guess I could send him to Alaska. But I swear, he'd run off and find his way back to his mama, no matter where I sent him. Has before. Three times. He thinks his daddy's gonna kill his mama if he isn't there. And I think he's right."

"You're not serious."

"Welcome to my world, honey. I can always get the dog put in jail. Just can't get him sent up the river for good, when the only witnesses keep lying in court. Anyhow… That's not what you're here for."

Lily admitted her visit was probably a lost cause. "I just wanted to ask if there was any chance the department kept records from twenty years ago."

"Honey, there are probably records in this place from the beginning of time. I can't give them to you without legal permission. But I can probably scare up what you want to know and then just tell you. What's the name, and what exactly are you looking for?"

Lily ran through the whole Campbell history. "I don't know if there's anything else we can find about the fire for sure, but there's been a question that has really troubled my sisters and me."

"And that is?"

"Why we were separated. We were orphaned by the fire, obviously, but each of us was fostered to different families, in different states. Can you tell me why that happened? I assume no one could afford to take on three kids? I realize how expensive that would have been. But I've been led to believe that my dad had some savings, so it's troubled all of us for a long time—why we were separated. And by such far distances."

"It is odd," Loreen agreed, and went on the hunt.

Old records and files had been computerized, but some of that historical data was saved on giant-sized floppies. Before reading them, they had to be converted and updated, which required a computer in a different room—which also required Loreen to order out for sandwiches, because she didn't miss lunch, and that was that. The phone rang, interrupting her several times, but Loreen repeated, "Just stay. We'll get our answers, and then we'll be done. It's not as if there'll be more time another day. There won't be. There never is."

In the meantime, Loreen kept up a general patter about Jason and Steven and Walter—and a half-dozen other boys that Griff had taken on. "Under the covers, you understand. Always under the covers. Doesn't foster. What he does is intervene, find some way for a boy in trouble to see another path. You can't always fix what's wrong. You can't make bad people into good. But youngsters, if they can see a way out, they're resilient. They're…well, shoot, honey."

"What?"

Loreen peered at the monitor, trying to read faded print on unclear copy. "I've got it. The report after your parents' fire. It was the sheriff."

"Pardon?"

"The sheriff was the one who advised the state that you three girls should be separated."

Lily sank in the battered office chair. "Sheriff Conner? But I've talked to him a bunch of times. He never said. Does it say why he advised that?"

"Hmm." Loreen scrolled through the document, which involved several pages of information. "Two families stepped up, said they'd take the three of you. But one was unsuitable—a farm. They really wanted child labor. Another, they only had a two-bedroom house, just wasn't big enough to add three youngsters. But that wasn't the problem. Apparently the social worker at the time—that'd be Samantha LaFitte, she retired around five years back, died last year—anyhow, she was the one who handled the case. Seems the sheriff's opinion was the one that pulled the weight."

"Why?" Lily repeated, feeling as if her world was being upended yet again.

All these years, her sisters could have been together?

And Herman Conner, who she'd talked to over and over, had hidden that information all this time?"

Loreen finally looked up again with a frown. "You need to understand. I'm no mighty fan of the law. I see injustice done to women and children every day. But I do think a lot of Sheriff Conner. He's never been the brightest knife in the drawer, but he had trouble with his own kids, never judged other people that I could see. He'll turn his back if he thinks it's the right thing. At least sometimes."

"I hear you. I thought he was a good guy, too."

"Apparently, he felt it was just the wrong thing for you three to stay in this town. He knew from personal experience that it was mighty hard for a child to live down a reputation. That an event or a problem could come back to haunt them. He thought it best if you three went somewhere where you'd make a completely clean start, forget about Pecan Valley altogether."

Loreen paged through to the end of the document, added, "Samantha LaFitte, she didn't agree. She apparently argued for you three to be together, wherever you landed. But the judge took the sheriff's advice. There's some comment here I can't quite read, but it refers to the sheriff having good reasons to understand problems with children."

Lily still had the oddest sinking sensation in her stomach. "What problems was that referring to?"

"I don't know, honey. Problems in his personal life, maybe, with his own kids? Or with kids in town? I wasn't in this job then. I always heard two of his girls were wild as teenagers, but really, I just don't know. Everybody always said he'd die for his kids. Was a great dad, a family man all the way. But that's all I know."

When Lily left the office, she walked out to a blaze of heat, immediately lifted the hair off her nape and hoped she'd survive walking the hundred feet to the rental car. For once though, her mind wasn't on whining about the Georgia summer. She was just plain confused.

There was nothing exactly wrong with the sheriff's play in the Campbell girls' future back then. It was the exact opposite of what the three sisters had wanted, but that didn't mean anything sinister or wrong or weird was involved. It just *felt* weird. That she'd talked to Herman Conner so many times, and he'd ducked any reference to his vote in their future back then.

She opened the car door, almost fell over from the blast of cooped up heat, and climbed in anyway. She dialed Griff on her cell, didn't reach him, left him a short message that she'd left social services and was headed for somewhere she could track down old high school yearbooks.

Surprisingly, Louella came up with that answer. Lily only popped back at the B and B to grab a notebook and change shoes, but Louella got talking, claimed that Susannah Danwell, who lived just three doors down— "She's over eighty, if she's a day, but still dressing like she's sixty-five, bless her heart, thinking she's fooling anyone. But she's been keeping the high school yearbooks forever. Wants to think of herself as a historian, she does, but the real truth is, her Herbert died, and she had nobody, so people come to visit her sometimes, to see the yearbooks, and she gets to talk then. She gets the company. I do wish she'd dress her age, but it's nothing to me, of course. Anyway, sugar, I'll call her and set it up, and you can take some of my caramel brownies over there, and it'll work like a charm. She'll be happy and you'll be happy, and it couldn't possibly work out any better...."

Lily knew Louella better than to interrupt—or to try arguing until Louella had finally run out of steam. Normally, Lily wouldn't have wanted to impose on a stranger, but Louella had dialed the number before she could stop her, told the infamous Susannah Danwell that Lily would be ambling over there in just a bit, and that she was a peach and a half.

"There now, honey, that's done. And you don't need to worry about a thing. I'll just call over there if there's any messages. That way, you can hole up and nobody'll know where you are, and you can just put your feet up with Susannah, bless her heart...."

Susannah, it turned out, lived in another of the city-styled antebellum homes. The veranda was long enough to bowl in, with a double screen door leading to a Scarlett O'Hara central staircase that gleamed with fresh polish. Her mother used to take in boarders, Susannah told her. She was dressed—as warned—with an I Love Vegas T-shirt and matching capris. Her neck, ears, wrists and arms glittered with rhinestones and bangles. "I do like a touch of elegance, honey, and oh, you have no idea how glad I am to meet you. The whole town's talking about what a wicked, wicked girl you are, and here, all I see is a little darling. Why, you're no bigger than a minute, are you? And you know what? I met your mama. And I was here when that fire happened, when the mill closed, all of it. Why, these caramel brownies are probably the best Louella ever baked. She dresses way too old for her years, bless her heart, but…"

Lily figured she'd never escape here until 2014— maybe—but as much as the older lady talked, she moved just as fast. Before much time passed, they were both sitting on a horsehair sofa, a lazy fan whirling overhead, and three high school year books opened on the crowded coffee table in front of them. Susannah had asked the year when her parents died, and picked that year and the two earlier ones to "peruse," as she put it.

"I don't exactly know what I'm looking for," Lily admitted. "I've picked up all kinds of new information, but nothing that pulls it all together."

"You want a 'bottom line,' as you young people like to say." Susannah licked her thumb, started peeling through pages. "You want proof your father didn't set the fire."

"Yes."

"And the proof would be if you found who *did* set that fire. You think someone in this age bracket set the other troublesome fires. The arson stories that were in the paper."

"Exactly. The person was never found, but all the evidence points to someone of high school age. A girl."

"Well, that only narrows it down by half," Susannah

said wryly. "I think we need a glass of sherry, don't you?"

Personally, Lily was no fan of sweet wines, but she couldn't turn down the older woman. Susannah was having a great time. She produced wineglasses "from a pawn shop in Reno."

"Real Irish crystal. Not that I'm a snob about such things. Oh, my…"

Lily scanned face after face, feeling increasingly foolish. She didn't know anyone, couldn't make any connection. But Susannah could, on every page.

"Oh, my heavens. Margo—you've met her, haven't you, the insurance agent? She had two nieces in high school, one after the other, both of them brighter than sunshine. The one made it all the way to her Ph.D., but sorry to say, the youngest got herself in the family way… never married, I hear…

"And there's Larry Wilson. Oh, what a heartthrob he was to the girls, every father's nightmare…Cashner Warden, I know you know him, the fire chief, he graduated a year ahead. He was another heartthrob back then, believe it or not. Quarterback of the football team. They lost every game. They were that bad. But he still looked good in that uniform, and there was always talk of the girls he was getting in trouble…oh my, oh my…"

Susannah clutched her chest with one hand—and reached over for the decanter of sherry with the other. Poured both of them another glass. "I'd forgotten. Our Herman Conner had five kids, you know, but there was one pair of twins, girls. He lost the one to a car accident when she was around fifteen. The whole family went to pieces, but especially her twin. Mary Belle ran around like a wild thing...you recognize her, don't you?"

"I do." The hairdresser with the wild, red hair.

"Well, the scandals about the girl near broke Herman's heart, but you know how it is. Some have to make mistakes their own way. She's turned into a good mama. Still hasn't got a lick of sense for men. But I think she still misses her sister, that something's always been missing for her...and oh, my, you know Debbie of Debbie's Diner? Well, her older brother..."

Lily sat straight.

She smelled it first. Just the barest whiff of smoke.

Followed by the distant scream of a fire truck engine.

"Oh my. Oh my." Susannah grabbed a chair arm and pushed to her feet. "I'm afraid that's close."

So was Lily. She shot out the door, leaving her purse, her papers, everything. Before she could fly down the steps of the veranda, the only sound in her head was a fierce, angry *no*.

She knew it was Louella's.

The bed and breakfast was the only other place in town where Lily had been that *hadn't* been targeted. But she thought, no one would do that to darling Louella. To that beautiful old house. Why? *Why?*

A car honked—she crossed the street without looking, running like a gazelle, seeing neighbors step outside, crossing arms, worried about what was happening, kids being called to come in from playing. Lily just kept charging ahead.

It wasn't the whole house. It was just one window

where clouds of thick, blustery smoke was starting to rumble out. *Her* window. The room *she* stayed in. Another measure she was to blame for this somehow, involved in this somehow, but if Louella was hurt, she'd never forgive herself.

She could hear the fire truck siren joined by police sirens, but neither rescue vehicle was in sight yet. A new boarder was standing on the front lawn when Lily leaped up the porch steps and slammed inside, calling Louella's name, not seeing her anywhere downstairs.

She took the stairs up two at a time, feeling the buildup of heat, her lungs whining at the choke of smoke. She found Louella in the hall, holding a handkerchief to her nose with one hand, trying to maneuver a heavy, unwieldy fire extinguisher with the other.

"Go!" Lily yelled at her.

Louella shook her head. "I'm not leaving my house!"

"I'll do it, Louella!" She grabbed the extinguisher, hefted it, pulled the pin and aimed the nozzle full bore. "If you have another extinguisher, get it. Or see if the neighbors have some."

"I—"

"I won't leave your fire until the firemen get here, I promise, Louella. But you go. Outside. Don't breathe this—" It was way too much talking. Both of them were starting to cough heavily, Louella bent over as she aimed for the stairs.

Lily turned back toward the bedroom, her eyes tearing in the rage of smoke—but she'd found the source. The wastebasket in her room was heaped with rags, reeked of gasoline. Fire danced up the lace curtains, shooting out the windows in scraps of seared lace and fabric. The white bedspread had caught a hem of fire now.

The extinguisher spewed foam, a white mousse that was almost as stinky as the fire. Lily kept aiming and shooting, her arms aching, screaming from holding the weight of the extinguisher.

"Lily!" Behind her, Louella had brought up another extinguisher. Lily took the fresh one, pulled the pin, let it rip.

"Go! Get out of the building!" she ordered the older woman.

"I am, I am. But the fire trucks. They just got here. So you can leave, too."

"I will! I will!" Yet she couldn't seem to desert the ship. She hadn't caused this, but she still felt responsible. The things burning up in front of her eyes—her yellow shorts, her cosmetic bag, her white sandals with the cork heels—they were already smoked and soaked and destroyed. But it hurt, sharp as a wound, that it was her stuff, her room that had been targeted.

The heat built. The smell and smoke increasingly choked her. She couldn't seem to get ahead of it. The bed pillow poofed, puffed, then came alive with fire, turning into a shower of sparks. The fire jumped, kept jumping. She put out curtains; then the lace scarf on the bureau sparked fresh. The old wallpaper on the far wall turned wet, shiny, started peeling.

The air seemed alive with moving, burning bits of debris. Clouds and wings of burning ash drifted in the air. Something tiny and sharp fell in her hair.

The burn was sharp and sudden. Instinctively, she dropped the extinguisher, batted at the pain in her head. Fear caught her like the sting of a whip. All these years she'd thought of fire as loss, as grief. Not as... personal. Not as something alive and lashing out. She spun, confused, choking, her palms stinging, her eyes blinded....

"Lily!"

Maybe she heard the fast thump of firemen's boots, the noise of voices. But the only thing she spun around for was the sound of Griff, calling her name.

She stumbled.

He caught her with a strong, sure grip. And with all the finesse of a tender lover, tossed a cold, soaking wet towel over her head.

The next stretch of time passed in a blur. Griff got her downstairs, set her up with a blanket in the front yard—and a medic. The medic was cute as a button, but it really, really hurt to have her palms cleaned, even though he talked to her nonstop. Jason hung tight to the periphery of her blanket like a scrawny, stubborn watchdog. Neighbors—some faces familiar, some not—clogged up the sidewalks and the yard.

Someone brought lemonade. Someone brought sweet tea. The party atmosphere built, completely at odds with the fire truck and official cars blocking the street. Louella, though, was holding court. Lily caught snatches of her conversation as the older lady poured lemonade and passed out spice cookies.

"See now? What did I tell you? She saved my house, she did. And Susannah'd be the first to tell you that she was at her house when this all happened. It's primarily Lily's things that were hurt. The child doesn't even have a change of clothes to wear. She's one of ours, has always been one of ours, and look at her now, bless her heart."

The medic, the one who had gorgeous blue eyes and looked about nine years old, finished putting salve and bandages on her palms and various other places, and then examined the side of her head. Shook his head.

"Not a pretty picture?" she asked.

"It's a gorgeous picture." Griff seemed to show up from nowhere—for the second time—and looked as covered in soot and dirt as she did. "Hair grows, besides."

"Uh-oh." When he came closer, she said quickly, "Don't come near me."

"Why?"

"I think I smell worse than anything I've smelled in my entire life."

He grinned. "Beneath all that fire and smoke, it's still you, sugar."

She remembered that. Remembered how his smooth soft lips had felt against hers. Remembered the sudden quiet of neighbors watching. Smiling. Griff...so *not* smiling.

Later, after talking to Cashner Warden and Herman Conner and Louella and Susannah—who had her purse and papers, thank heavens—Griff took her home. She seemed to need to cough her lungs out several times. Jason was there. He had ideas—like ice cream. Lots of cool, soothing ice cream. He thought she needed to watch a nice, soothing movie, an old one, like *Batman,* or *The Fantastic Four.*

But Jason wasn't there when Griff lowered her into a bathtub. He'd started by sealing up her hands in bags with rubber bands, so the water wouldn't touch the burns on her palms. Kneeling behind her, he washed her hair, washed her face, washed her toes, washed everything, slowly, carefully, tenderly. Silently.

"You know what I figured out?" she asked him.

"What?"

"That it's about anger. Setting these fires. It's not about destruction. Even those fires years ago didn't actually destroy that much property. Or specifically aim to hurt a human being. It's all about anger. Someone with a rage that's just out of their control."

When Griff said nothing—he was spraying water to rinse her hair at the time—she waited until she could open her eyes to look at him. Really look at him.

"I think I'm a little in shock," she admitted.

"I know you are."

"I'm afraid I'll have to go shopping tomorrow. I'm down to today's clothes. Which aren't exactly fit for man or beast." When she couldn't win a smile from him, she said, "In the background, I thought I heard Louella saying that insurance would cover the damage. Completely."

"There was an insurance agent right there. Won't be a problem."

"I'll need to borrow a toothbrush until tomorrow."

"No sweat."

"And from the way people have been looking at me, I'm afraid I'm definitely going to have to work in a haircut tomorrow, too."

Again, that same expression in his eyes. What few

words he said were short and curt, even as his hands, his magic hands, lingered as he soaped and rinsed, and finally, let her stand up so he could fold a towel around her.

"Griff."

He looked up.

"What's wrong?"

"What's wrong?" he echoed, his tone tight as a snap. But then he went back to his lazy, laid-back tone. "You're going to take a nap, sugar. Nothing's wrong. Everything's going to be one hundred percent fine."

"You know this how?"

"Because tomorrow—we're getting to the bottom of this. Whatever sabers we have to rattle. Whatever it takes. You're not going to be hurt again. There aren't going to be any more fires. You can take it to the bank, we're solving this once and for all."

Lily heard the anger in his voice, and loved it—not that he was worried about her, but that he finally felt free with her, to let out that unsettling anger that so troubled him.

Yet her heart suddenly twisted in a totally unexpected knot. She, too, had had it with fires. She had had it with exhaustion and fear and worry. She thought she'd come to this town of her childhood to find answers.

Yet the irony hurt worse than any burn. If, by any chance, she and Griff did find the answers, her reasons for being in Pecan Valley disappeared.

She had no more reason to be with Griff.

No reason to stay.

Chapter 12

Lily woke up in a first-class grump, starting with the note on her pillow. Griff unwillingly had to return Jason to his mother, at least temporarily, and then he was headed for the sheriff's.

He wanted her to rest and sit tight.

Right.

One look in the mirror sent her jogging for a phone. Her singed hair looked like something out of a horror movie. No matter what she wanted to do with her day, she was stuck getting a few chores out of the way first. As often as she'd ranted about getting a haircut since she got here, now she had no choice but to call Mary Belle. The sheriff's daughter promised her she'd clear the schedule for ll:30—leaving Lily enough time to run through a few stores on Main Street.

Temporarily, she had nothing to wear but a shirt and

shorts from Griff, which no amount of makeshift belting was going to pass for acceptable clothes. She had her purse, so at least she had a brush and lip gloss—and her phone. She'd barely headed out the door before getting the first barrage of calls from her sisters.

"I'll send you money. Get all the clothes you need," Cate started with. "And buy a first-class ticket to me. I don't care what it costs. You either get out of that town, or I'm flying there to get you myself."

Sophie's call was more of the same, just in a softer tone.

The truth was, Lily hungered to see both her sisters. And she could hardly stay in Pecan Valley much longer. Once, her answers had seemed terribly important to her—but not as important as a whole town burning up because of her. Leaving needed to be her priority. It was just…leaving town also meant leaving Griff.

How a woman could fall so fast, so hard, so irrevocably, she couldn't fathom. For her whole life, it had been so, so easy to stay untangled. She'd never risked loss—at least the kind of loss where the hurt might never really heal.

Damn it. How was she supposed to forget Griff?

Most stores on Main Street opened at ten. It took almost that long to pull herself together, between her bandaged hands and edgy mood. Clouds were bunching and punching overhead, threatening rain, adding humidity to an already gasping temperature. She hit the drugstore first, picked up the obvious toiletries, like deodorant and toothpaste and cosmetics, then stashed those in her car.

There were several clothing stores and boutiques on

Main Street. She didn't have a clue what they offered. She just wanted to pick up enough basics to wear for a few days. So she started with the first one—Jane's Boutique, the sign said. Opening the door set off a tinkling bell, and almost immediately she panicked.

It wasn't a day to be fussy, but the manikins were decked out in bows and prints and polka dots. She almost headed straight back out, but the thirtyish brunette behind the cash register spotted her and immediately approached with a smile. "You have to be Lily Campbell. I see those hurt hands, you poor thing. The whole town's buzzing with how you helped saved Louella's house and Louella…come in, come in. I'll help you. I can see you can't do much with those hands. I'll bet they hurt like the devil?"

They did. Everything seemed to hurt like the devil— but it did help, coming in town today, being greeted everywhere, so far, with smiles instead of suspicion. Jane didn't do much talking, but behind her pretty eyes was a shrewd saleswoman. Packages on the counter added up. No bows, no doodads. A white lace bra, a navy satin one. Matching underwear. A sundress in pale blues. A breezy skirt and cami that could go to dinner, or just about anywhere else. A coral top, cream shorts—those she decided to wear, with Jane's help.

The shop had earrings, bangles, shoes, bags, all the "stuff" to put it altogether. Lily didn't intend to buy so much—if she was flying home, she just didn't need that much from here. But Jane seemed to sort through the fussy stuff and come through with exactly what Lily liked, and it all added up. When she headed back out, her arms were heaped with packages, and naturally, by then it was pouring. She only had minutes to stash the clothes in her rental car and dash through the rain to the hair salon.

To her surprise, the only body in Mary Belle's was Mary Belle—who appeared to be pacing in front of the storefront windows when Lily ran in. "I told everyone to take a two-hour lunch break," she greeted her with. "Give us some time to chat. And I didn't want anyone handling you but me."

It was a kindly thing to say—but somehow Lily felt a sudden shiver. Of course, she was damp at the edges from her run through the rain, and the salon was more than cool. The shop looked like its owner. No soothing décor for Mary Belle; she'd opted for bright slashes of orange and yellow, seats in shiny purple.

"I don't need much. Just a trim," Lily said immediately.

"You need way more than a trim, honey. That fire sure singed you on one side, didn't it? But don't you worry. You'll look like a new woman before I'm through with you."

Again, Lily felt a frisson of unease. It was stupid. The mix of air-conditioning and intense humidity were creating the chill, nothing else.

She followed the other woman to the back, where Mary Belle wrapped her in a wild polka-dot cape and motioned her to the hair washing chair.

"You're going to love this," she informed Lily. Which was the truth. It was impossible not to love the scalp rub, the massage of warm water and fragrant shampoo products.

"I love this place," Mary Belle said conversationally, yet there was the oddest tone in her voice. Regret? Sadness? "I built the shop from scratch, all on my own. Was never much of a student in high school. Not one of those college-bound types of girls. I always attracted the boys, of course, with my looks. But all they ever did was break my heart, and leave me pregnant with the bills for divorce. This place...this was all mine. I never let a man's name get on it. If it were my choice, I'd never let a man through the door."

Lily's eyes were closed as Mary Belle rinsed out the shampoo, then massaged in conditioner with expert hands.

"It's a wonderful place," Lily said, for lack of anything better to comment.

"It'll kill me to lose it."

Lily assumed she'd misheard her. The comment made no sense—but the water was running, the conditioner being rinsed out, then a towel plopped on her head and the seat raised.

"Now for the trim," Mary Belle said. "And I do promise. You're going to get the trim of your life."

Fear dried Lily's throat. It was the stress, she told herself. She wasn't thinking clearly. Even if somehow she found out the arsonist from all those years ago, even if that same female arsonist was the one who caused her parents' fire, it wasn't going to be someone who'd openly talked to her from the day she arrived in Pecan Valley.

It wasn't going to be the sheriff's daughter. How crazy was that?

Mary Belle pumped the chair higher, then tied the long plastic cape tighter around Lily's neck. The scissors suddenly gleamed inches from her eyes.

"I saw your picture in the yearbook," Lily blurted out.

"Yeah? I was quite a looker, wasn't I?"

"You still are," Lily assured her.

"There's no point trying to be nice now, honey. It's too late. I knew when you got into town that it could all come crashing down if I wasn't absolutely careful. But I swear, you are the *dumbest* woman. You could have left after the first fire. After the second. But no, you had to keep digging and digging and digging."

Snip, snip, snip. Lily saw the snips of hair fall. Then hanks of it. About the same second she froze up with panic, she realized that Mary Belle hadn't just tied the cape around her—but around the chair as well. She could move her legs. She could move her bandaged hands under the cape. But she couldn't get out of the chair.

"Don't be squirming around now. I don't want these scissors to slip accidentally. Don't worry. I'll make you look good. You're going to be last customer, and I want your hair cut to look just right."

"Mary Belle—"

"The place will go up fast. Losing this place is going to kill me, like I said. But by the time the firemen get here, I'll be out in the street, screaming for help, and you'll be the only one inside. They'll think you set yet another fire, Lily. And that this one finally got you, too.

I never wanted it to be this way, I swear," she said sadly. "But something I want you to know…"

"What?" Lily had stopped breathing. Her gaze tracked the movement of the scissors, her mind racing, trying to find a way out. Trying to think of a way out.

"Your parents, they were never supposed to die. I felt terrible about that. No one was ever supposed to get hurt, not physically—whoa there, bless your heart. That was silly, your trying to move. You're not going anywhere."

The tip of the scissors nicked Lily's neck, right at the throat. A thin crimson line shone in the mirror.

"We're not done with this haircut," Mary Belle told her. "And believe me, you don't want me to rush." She turned the chair, so Lily had a view of the products on the counter. "See there?"

Mutely, Lily looked. The counter of products hadn't caught her attention before, but there was nothing she wouldn't expect to see in a hair salon. But now she realized that Mary Belle had set up an altar. The hair sprays and potions, the nail polishes and nail polish removers, all had their tops opened, and were arranged prettily with a candle in the center.

Only one other item was included in the display. A hairdryer. A plain old, standard salon hairdryer—except that the back had been removed, revealing the naked heating coils.

Mary Belle smoothly plugged in the hairdryer, at the same time she spun around and competently, swiftly, wrapped adhesive tape round and round Lily, the cape trapping her arms and upper torso. "It'll be a little while before those coils heat up. We're not done with the haircut. And I need a few more minutes to brace myself before losing my shop. This is the one thing I valued in the world besides my daughters and my daddy. So don't be feeling sorry for yourself, because I'm gonna lose a lot here, too. If you'd just never come back, this never would have happened. It's your fault. Everything's your fault."

As if they were discussing the weather, Mary Belle looked at her haircut creation in the mirror, from one angle and then another. "I believe we'll go just a little shorter on the left side, don't you think?"

All Lily could think was, *Griff.* The one man she definitely wanted to love and live for, not die for.

The coils on the bald hair dryer started to glow....

When Griff dropped into the creaking office chair in Sheriff Conner's office, he stretched out his long legs, calm as a spring breeze. "We need to have a little discussion," he said lazily, and accepted the mug of battery-acid strength coffee that Herman Conner pushed toward him.

"Now, Griff. There's no point in your getting mad over that boy."

"I'm not mad. I never get mad," Griff assured him. He realized Conner thought he was unhappy about Jason being returned to his mother's house. And he was. But the dominating headlines in his mind were the images of Lily's soot-stained cheeks and shocked eyes after yesterday's fire.

At three in the morning, he'd still been pacing the

floor, checking on her every five minutes, leaping up every time she coughed.

And since he hadn't gotten a lick of sleep, he'd put all the information they'd gathered on the Campbell fire in his head. It was like watching puzzle pieces interlock. They knew someone had committed three or more acts of arson twenty years ago. That that someone was likely a girl. That that someone had gotten away with her crimes—and the only reason Lily's appearance in town had started a rash of arson fires was if the guilty person then was the guilty person now.

If there was another way to put it together, Griff didn't know how. What he'd realized, in the wee hours of the morning, was that someone else had all the puzzle pieces he and Lily had. Maybe more.

And that someone was the sheriff.

"Here's the thing." Conner poured himself a second mug, pulled out a drawer, propped his boot on it. "You and I know the score on kids like Jason. You're too realistic to think there's ever some magic answer for a troubled kid."

"I don't. But if Jason's father wasn't a relative of the judge, you know damn well he'd be in prison, instead of getting a free ride out of jail every few months."

"True. But that's one of the things you can't change. So you either eat yourself up about it, or you do what you can do." Conner tipped back his chair. "I don't know if you're aware of this, but I had five kids of my own. Two of them nearly cost my sanity. That's how I know. All you can do is what you can do, Griff."

Griff suddenly rubbed an itch at the back of his neck. "Which two kids? What happened?"

The sheriff sighed. "I had twins. Twin girls. And when Mary Ann died in an accident, I thought my wife would sink under the weight of it. She just couldn't recover. I had a hard enough time myself. Nothing shook us out of that grief until we finally noticed that Mary Belle...well, let's just say, she was barreling down the wrong path."

"How so?" Griff asked lazily.

The sheriff's eyes shifted away from him. "What I think now is that losing her sister, her twin, just rocked Mary Belle's foundation to the core. It's like she was trying to believe she didn't care about losing her sister, about herself, about anything. She turned into this wild girl, out of control every which way."

"I take it she partied quite a bit?"

Conner took another pull on the coffee. "To say the least of it." He sighed again. "I blame myself for not paying attention. We were too wrapped up in our own grief to see it. She was wildly in love with a new boy about every month. It's not as if a high school boy is going to say no when something's offered free."

"Not in this life," Griff affirmed, although his pulse was suddenly slamming, slamming, slamming.

"So each of the boys she took up, they took advantage. And then they'd break her heart. Then she'd get so angry. And even more wild." Conner shook his head. "The thing is, when I see a boy like Jason, or Steve, or any of the wild-eyed ones you've taken on...I always remember what we been through in our own family. You can love your kids. You can try to parent them right. But sometimes problems come up that just plain take time, a lot of time, to turn around."

Griff said quietly, softly, "So…it was Mary Belle, wasn't it? Who set those fires twenty years ago."

"Say what? I was talking about the nature of teenagers, kids through times of trouble, how sometimes raising a kid just isn't a neat, tidy, straight path—"

"She set the fires, didn't she, Conner."

The sheriff shook his head wildly, slammed his feet flat on the floor. "I don't know what you're talking about. "I only brought up my own family issues to share your frustration over Jason. I wasn't trying to—"

Griff could see it in Conner's face. The anguish. The guilt. Likely he would never have mentioned Mary Belle, his own troubles, if his daughter wasn't such a huge, festering worry in his mind that he couldn't always keep in.

"In high school. The arson fires that were never solved," he said quietly. "She was in love with those boys. They took advantage, then jilted her. She was angry. She set those fires."

"No, of course it wasn't her!"

"Only then came the fire that killed the Campbells. Lily's parents." Griff eased to his feet, then crossed the room to quietly close the door. When he turned back, Conner's ruddy complexion had gone gray, his eyes old. He lifted a hand to push it through his rumpled hair. The hand was trembling. He realized it. Griff saw it.

"It's not like you think," the sheriff said.

"So tell me how it was."

"I didn't know it was her. Not to start. It never occurred

to me in a million years that it was my own daughter. " Once Conner started talking, it was as if a raw, festering boil had suddenly exploded.

"After her sister died, she just went searching for something, you know? She'd decide she loved some boy, sleep with him, probably scare the boy out of his mind with how fast and furious she was latching on. So he'd dump her. And then there'd be a fire."

"Aw, hell." Griff said it under his breath. He hadn't known, not totally, not for dead sure, until the sheriff let loose.

"I didn't associate those fires with Mary Belle. Why would I? At first I thought it was just vandalism. First one was in a school locker. I thought, probably pranks, a sports rivalry. It's boys who set fires, almost never girls. And our Mary Belle, we were worried about her morals. But we weren't worried about *crime,* certainly nothing like those fires. She'd never done anything like that, never got in any kind of trouble—"

"Why in God's name did she pick on the Campbells?"

"She didn't. But she was pregnant. I didn't know. Her mother didn't know. The house next to Campbells was empty, for sale. That's where she and this boy were meeting at night. He had a way of getting in. Anyway she told him she was pregnant. Thought he'd marry her, they'd live happy ever after. He dumped her, called her a slut, said the only reason he was with her was for one thing…."

"And?"

"When the fire happened, when the Campbells died,

I still didn't know it was her. Nobody did. But she came crying to me, beside herself, guilty, ashamed, torn up. She never meant to hurt anyone else. She didn't even mean to hurt *him*. She'd never harmed a person."

Griff almost responded, realized every muscle in his spine was knotted tighter than barbed wire, and said nothing. Conner, he was pretty damned positive, had never told anyone about this. It had eaten him alive all this time.

"I'd do anything for my kids, you understand? I'd throw myself in front of a bus if I had to. When that fire happened—when she finally broke and told me—the Campbells, they were already gone. Nothing could save them. Nothing could make that right."

"And you thought that made it okay to do nothing?" Griff had to keep the growl from his voice.

"No. Hell, no. But bringing it all to light was only going to ruin my daughter's life, too—as well as the child's in her belly. Her guilt, her responsibility, was to turn her life around. And she did that. She really did that. No, she didn't make good marriages. But she's been a good, fine mother. She pays her bills. She doesn't play around at all anymore. She may look like she does, but she's got her lights out at nine, just like her kids. She works hard, built that salon from scratch—"

Griff heard the word *salon* and a bullet went off in his head. He whirled around, grabbed the doorknob.

"What?" Conner said. "Where are you going?"

Adrenaline shot through Griff's veins. Lily had babbled last night about getting some clothes, getting the soot and singe cut from her hair. Maybe there was another salon. It wasn't as if Griff kept track of the women hairstylists in town. But the only one Lily had actually met was Mary Belle.

"What?" Conner repeated from behind him. "What are you doing? Where are you going?"

"I think Lily's with your daughter. Right now."

He didn't look back to see what the sheriff did, he just ran.

He pushed through doors, down steps, past people. Torrents of rain bounced on the pavement, soaking him through before he'd made it a hundred yards. He passed his car—and yeah, it was right there—but to get three blocks, he could run faster, and did.

Enough had happened in the last three weeks to make the whole town jumpy. Griff running down Main Street attracted faces in windows, doors opening, a buzz of worried questions—and bodies in his way. He ducked and dodged, thinking that Lily had run through almost nine lives since she got here, but he was the one who wouldn't survive if she wasn't totally, completely all right.

He couldn't be too late.

He couldn't be.

Blinds were drawn on the salon windows; a sign at the door claimed the shop was closed for a few hours. That stopped him less than a second. Maybe the door was locked; if so, a sharp twist and push and it gave. He stepped in, had a heart attack. Damn near tripped over Mary Belle, who for some insane reason was curled on the floor crying her eyes out.

Lily was in a salon chair. Trapped. Tape circled her

a half dozen times and her mouth was taped shut. Her eyes, her gorgeous eyes, were spitting tears—fear, rage, pain? In that first instant, he couldn't grasp what was happening, the source of danger.

Lily made a muffled sound, bobbed her head over and over to the left. He crossed the room in long strides, saw in that single blink where she was trying to motion him…a hairdryer, plugged in, but the back off, revealing red-hot coils.

Then he got it. The counter of explosive products.

He yanked the plug, grabbed the dryer, heaved it into the farthest sink basin—traveling over the crazy heap of crying Mary Belle a second time. Then back to Lily. He ripped off the tape, heard her hoarsely cry his name. Then ripped at the tape wrapping her, unwinding it, his fingers fumbling blind, his gaze on her face, her lips, her eyes.

When he'd loosened all the miles of tape enough for her to break loose, she more than broke free, hurling herself up and into his arms.

His voice came out in rusty threads. "Damn stupid time to tell you, but I love you more than life." More rust. His throat felt that raw. "I *told* you not to get a haircut here."

"I know." Her face lifted to his. She had to hear—so did he—the building commotion behind them. Bodies coming in. People talking. The sheriff's voice. All he could see or hear was Lily. She took in a heave of a breath, a gulp of a sob. He soothed his fingers in her short hair, touching her, holding her, wanting to shield her. From everything. From now on. Forever.

"You won't believe what stopped her," she said. "Her youngest daughter telephoned. Mary Belle was all set to blow it up. To blow *me* up. And her daughter was just calling to ask about a spaghetti recipe or something that silly, and just hearing her daughter's voice—that was it. Suddenly she caved. Curled up in that ball, started crying and couldn't stop. Started rocking. But the coils on that hair dryer, Griff. They were hot. They were so red-hot. Another few minutes and…"

"Griff? Lily?"

A fire truck screamed from the street—this time, thank God, not needed—but Pecan Valley wasn't going to risk not being ready ever again. A man's hand cuffed his shoulder, trying to get his attention.

Griff wanted to get her out of here. Knew there were things that needed doing, saying, knowing. But for that instant, he just needed to breathe her in a little longer. Feel her hair, her skin. The frantic pulse in her throat was finally easing, that shocky glaze in her eyes softening. Her lips parted.

"You can't mean it," she said.

"Mean what?"

"That you're in love with me. I mean…I know. We've been…two. I know we have something, are something when we're together. But I told you it was all right, Griff."

"Nothing's been all right since you got here."

"Which will make it easy for you to forget me."

"Which will make it *impossible* for me to forget you," he corrected her. "You're going to have to give it up. Lily. Pretending you're into flings. You're not into affairs. You're into *me*. The same hot, dangerous, risky, impossibly way I'm into you. And frankly, I'm expecting to be into you—"

"Through fire and smoke?" she whispered.

"Hey. We already know we can survive that part."

Her lips curved on the start of a smile. It was all he needed to see. He ducked his head, sealed his mouth on hers. He closed his eyes and just took her in. The promise in her lips, the hope in how they fit together, the release of a lonely heart letting go. For her. With her.

Then, of course, they both lifted their heads. And turned together to face whatever questions needed answering, whatever issues needed resolving and explaining. Together.

Epilogue

Ten Days Later

"All right, you." Lily slid open the shower door, put her hands on her hips. "I've been looking all *over* for you."

"I had to get some work done."

"Yeah, right. In the shower."

He looked up guiltily from his laptop. "I admit, I never tried setting up an office in the shower before. But your sisters are a little…"

"Petrifying?"

"They're adorable," he assured her. "And I like their choice of men. Both of them, more than good guys. Interesting, bright. But your sisters—"

"Come on. I know you like them."

"I do. I do. It's just that the grilling is nonstop. So are the orders. You can't live in a hot climate. Anyone who hurts you will endure a not-very-pretty death. Expect high phone bills, you three talk every week. You've all been through hell, but they both say you were hurt the worst. A lifetime of my pampering you isn't enough or close to enough. Jewels aren't enough—"

"Okay. I get the picture." Truthfully, she'd primarily tracked him down to empathize. She knew what her sisters had put him through. He'd been a brick. But she needed some time alone with Griff, and totally understood how he felt.

"Your oldest sister—Cate—hey, she should be in Special Forces, particularly in interrogation. She would have followed me into the bathroom if I'd let her. When she wants to know something, she just doesn't let up. And then there's Sophie—she flashes those big, soft eyes and you think she's sweet. She's not. She's a pit bull with a soft voice."

"You poor baby."

"At least they like my ice cream. But a locked door doesn't keep Cate out of anything, does it? Nor Sophie. Neither of them have ever heard of privacy."

Lily winced. "Not where I'm concerned, I'm afraid." Of course, he was the one who'd invited both her sisters—and their husbands. And insisted that everyone stay at his place. Lily was willing to feel a little sorry for him, but not too much. Particularly when he was hamming up the long-suffering tone. "I had to search you out for a reason."

"Because you wanted to take a shower with me?"

"You know I do. But not right this minute." She took

a breath. "Two calls came in. One from the district attorney. The other from Sheriff Conner."

Griff immediately closed down his laptop and stood up, all teasing gone from his voice. "What's the news?"

"No trial."

"*What?* Don't tell me they're letting her get off scot-free—"

"Now, Griff. Don't let your temper get away from you—"

"I have no temper. I've told you a zillion times."

He had no temper he'd vent on her. She had no doubt about that whatsoever. She put a hand on his chest, hoping to calm his suddenly galloping heartbeat. "I was happy with this, Griff. There's been enough loss and hardship. She has two young daughters. What happens to them is part of this picture. So she'll plead guilty and do a plea bargain. There'll have to be some time done, but possibly locally. And she'll have to participate in several years of intensive counseling, do community service for more years than that."

She felt his eyes on her face, searching, trying to read her. "You sure you're all right with this?"

"I'm not sure there is an 'all right' for this kind of thing. She's to blame for our parents dying. That's not easy to let go of, even if she never dreamed that could happen. But her intent does matter. She was young. She was messed up. She'd never figured out the loss of her sister, why she went looking for love in the wrong places, what all that anger of hers was about. But she stopped at the salon, Griff. She heard her daughter's voice on the phone, felt that love for her daughter, and she stopped."

Griff wasn't ready to be so forgiving. "The whole place could still have blown up—"

"Yes. And that's still on her head. But I don't see how it solves anything to wipe the floor with her. I want there to be a penalty, yes. Costs, yes. But nothing's going to really change until she understands how those screws got loose. She's got a daughter, a father, siblings. I'll be darned if I want to be part of separating another family, Griff."

"And is that what your sisters think?"

"I haven't told them. I told you first. I was hoping you'd come with me to share it all."

"Sure."

"Even if you *don't* agree with me, I *want* you to agree with me," she said firmly.

He shook his head. "The fact that I understand what you just said is frightening. I think it's a sign we should get married, Lily."

It was her turn for her heart to stop. "Is that a proposal?"

"Good grief no. You're not getting a formal question until your sisters are long, long gone. Just for the record, I did happen to pick out a ring. But it's a box that I'm afraid you can't open until we're in Vancouver."

Odd, how her heart not only restarted, but suddenly picked up a luscious, sweet speed. "Vancouver?"

"Yeah. I don't know if you'll want to live there, But doing the proposal there would give us a good excuse to check it out. It's nice and cool. Your kind of climate.

I know a place…high up. Overlooking the water. Big white feather beds and giant Adirondack chairs on the balcony. Lobster for lunch. Love for dinner. How does that sound so far?"

She took his hands, looked up at him. It was still hard for her to accept it, to believe it—the love in his eyes, the absolute sureness. Griff was so un-self-aware. He really believed he was laid-back, when he wasn't remotely. She loved everything about him, from the way he was with kids, to how hard he fought to repress any hint of temper, to his dedication in everything he took on, to everything he did….

He'd be a good man to hunker down with, she knew. On a cold winter night, setting a fire with him was the best dream she could imagine. Not the kind of fire that hurt.

But the kind of fire that burned, from the inside out. The kind of fire that came from the heart. The kind of fire that made babies, that made a family, that protected and sealed and warmed.

"Lily," he murmured. "You're scaring me to death. Could I have an answer?"

"Yes!" she said clearly. "Yes, to everything. Yes to loving you, Griff. Yes to being with you all the days of our lives. Yes to—"

His kiss interrupted all the yesses she was about to offer him.

She'd have to get the rest in just a wee bit later.

* * * * *

COMING NEXT MONTH

Available December 28, 2010

ROMANTIC SUSPENSE

SRSCNM1210

REQUEST YOUR FREE BOOKS!

2 FREE NOVELS PLUS 2 FREE GIFTS!

ROMANTIC *SUSPENSE*

Sparked by Danger, Fueled by Passion.

SRS10R

HARLEQUIN®

A Romance

FOR EVERY MOOD™

Spotlight on

Classic

Quintessential, modern love stories
that are romance at its finest.

See the next page
to enjoy a sneak peek from
the Harlequin Presents® series.

"LET ME GET THIS STRAIGHT. Are you actually suggesting that I would stoop to that kind of game playing?"

Saul came out from behind his desk and walked toward her. Giselle could smell his hot male scent and it was making her dizzy, igniting a low, dull, pulsing ache that was taking over her whole body.

Giselle defended her suspicions. "You don't want me here."

"No," Saul agreed, "I don't."

And then he did what he had sworn he would not do, cursing himself beneath his breath as he reached for her, pulling her fiercely into his arms and kissing her with all the pent-up fury she had aroused in him from the moment he had first seen her.

Giselle certainly *wanted* to resist him. But the hand she raised to push him away developed a will of its own and was sliding along his bare arm beneath the sleeve of his shirt, and the body that should have been arching away from him was instead melting into him.

Beneath the pressure of his kiss he could feel and taste her gasp of undeniable response to him. He wanted to devour her, take her and drive them both until they were equally satiated—even whilst the anger within him that she should make him feel that way roared and burned its resentment of his need.

She was helpless, Giselle recognized, totally unable to withstand the storm lashing at her, able only to cling to the man who was the cause of it and pray that she would survive.

Somewhere else in the building a door banged. The sound exploded into the sensual tension that had enclosed them, driving them apart. Saul's chest was rising and falling as he fought for control; Giselle's whole body was trembling.

Without a word she turned and ran.

Find out what happens when Saul and Giselle succumb to their irresistible desire in

THE RELUCTANT SURRENDER

Available January 2011 from Harlequin Presents®

Silhouette Desire

HAVE BABY,
NEED BILLIONAIRE

MAUREEN CHILD

Simon Bradley is accomplished, successful and very proud. The fact that he has to prove he's fit to be a father to his own child is preposterous. Especially when he has to prove it to Tula Barrons, one of the most scatterbrained women he's ever met. But Simon has a ruthless plan to win Tula over and when passion overrules prudence one night, it opens up the door to an affair that leaves them both staggering. Will this billionaire bachelor learn to love more than his fortune?

Billionaires and Babies

Available January
wherever books are sold.

Always Powerful, Passionate and Provocative.